As you enter the apartment, ... wall. Neither of us had as ... wall. I thought of book-she... a good copy of a modern pa... time arguing about this, a... was going to get her way.

As I entered the apartment, I was no longer confronted by the blank wall.

Instead, scrawled in aerosol paint in six-inch letters was the message:

KEEP AWAY FROM ANGIE OR ELSE.

He must have been waiting for me behind the front door. He was quick and very expert. I just heard the swish of a descending sap, then saw flashes of light, then there was a complete blackout . . .

JAMES HADLEY CHASE

'If you want entertainment you could scarcely do better'
The Times

'Master of the art of deception'
New Statesman

'The way he builds up a plot, layer upon layer, is so effective'
Bernard Levin *Sunday Times*

'I always enjoy his books . . . He just keeps me reading'
George Macdonald Fraser

By the same author

JAMES HADLEY CHASE

Hit Them Where it Hurts

GRAFTON BOOKS
A Division of the Collins Publishing Group

LONDON GLASGOW
TORONTO SYDNEY AUCKLAND

Grafton Books
A Division of the Collins Publishing Group
8 Grafton Street, London W1X 3LA

Published by Grafton Books 1985
Reprinted 1986, 1987, 1990

First published in Great Britain by
Robert Hale Limited 1984

Copyright © James Hadley Chase 1984

ISBN 0-586-06086-3

Printed and bound in Great Britain by
Collins, Glasgow

Set in Plantin

1

My name is Dirk Wallace: unmarried, pushing 40 years of age, tall, dark, with a face that, so far, doesn't frighten the kiddies. I am one of the twenty operators working for the Acme Detective Agency which is housed on the top floor of the Trueman Building, Paradise Avenue, Paradise City, Florida.

The Acme Detective Agency is the most expensive and best agency on the east coast of the USA. Founded by Colonel Victor Parnell, a Vietnam war veteran, some six years ago, the agency had prospered. Parnell had been smart enough to realize that sooner or later many of the billionaires living in Paradise City would need the services of a top-class detective agency. The agency specialized in divorce, parents' problems, blackmail, extortion, hotel swindles, husband and wife watching, and pretty near everything short of mayhem and murder.

The twenty operators, most of us ex-cops or ex-military police, work in pairs. Each pair has an office, and unless there is an emergency, the operators know nothing about the work done by their colleagues. This system is to prevent leaks to the press. Should there be a leak, and it happened once, both operators working on the case are given the gate.

Having worked for the agency for the past eighteen months I had been promoted and given an office of my own, but my assistant, ex-Deputy-Sheriff Bill Anderson, also had a desk in my office.

Bill Anderson was pint-size, but he had plenty of muscle and beef around his shoulders. He had been a big help to me sorting out a tricky case when I had been sent to Searle to find a missing youngster. Then he had been deputy sheriff and was longing to join the agency. Because of his help I had cracked the case*, and in return I got him into the agency.

In every way Bill Anderson proved invaluable to me. He didn't care what hours he worked, and in this racket this is important. He was top class at ferreting out information I needed, saving me dreary hours of research. When we weren't working, he explored the city, and became an expert on restaurants, night-clubs and the lower strata of the waterfront. The toughs, to their cost, ignored him because of his size. Tiny as he is, his punch would knock over an elephant.

This morning in July we were sitting in my office, waiting for action. It was raining and humid. Only the elderly residents remained in the city: the rich visitors and the tourists waited until September.

Anderson, chewing gum, was writing a letter home. With my feet on my desk, I was thinking of Suzy.

She and I had met some six months ago, and we had liked each other on sight.

Suzy Long was a receptionist at the Bellevue Hotel. I had made an enquiry about a creep, staying there, who was a suspected blackmailer. Once I had explained the set-up to Suzy, she was helpful, and I got enough evidence to pass to the cops, and the creep got five years in the slammer.

Suzy had long, glossy brown hair with a hint of red in her tresses, grey eyes and a lively, almost mischievous smile. She was built the way I liked girls to be built: full-breasted, tiny waist, voluptuous hips and long legs. We got together, and now had a standing date for dinner at a modest sea-food restaurant every Wednesday night when she had a night off from the hotel. After eating, we went back to her tiny apartment and rolled together on her rather too small bed. This went on for three months or so, then we both realized we were really in love with each other. During my life as an

* See *Hand Me A Fig Leaf*.

operator I had had a score of women, but now Suzy meant more to me than any other woman. I suggested it could be an idea for us to get married. She had given her mischievous smile, shaking her head. 'Not yet, Dirk,' she had said. 'I like the idea, but I have a good, well paid job, and if I married you I would have to give it up. Your hours of work and mine just don't jell. Not yet, my love, but later.'

I had to be content with that, so, today being Wednesday, I was thinking of the fun she and I would have tonight, when my intercom buzzed.

I turned the switch down and said, 'Wallace.'

'Will you come to my office, please?' I recognized Glenda Kerry's harsh voice.

Glenda Kerry was the colonel's secretary and right hand. Tall, good-looking, dark, she was alarmingly efficient. When she said, 'Come,' you went.

I walked fast down the long corridor to her office. The colonel was away in Washington. Glenda was in charge. I tapped on her door, entered to find her at her desk, looking immaculate in white blouse and black skirt.

'An assignment has come in,' she said as I sat down, facing her. 'Mrs Henry Thorsen telephoned. She wants an operator to call on her at twelve this morning when she will explain her requirements. She asked for an intelligent, decently dressed man.'

'So you immediately thought of me,' I said.

'I thought of you because all operators except you have cases,' Glenda said curtly. 'Does the name Henry Thorsen mean anything to you?'

I shrugged.

'Can't say it does. Is he important?'

Glenda sighed.

'He is dead. Mrs Thorsen has been a widow for a year. She is extremely wealthy and has a lot of clout. Handle her with kid gloves. All I can tell you is she's difficult. Go, find out what she wants.' She pushed a slip of paper across her desk. 'That's her address. Be there at twelve sharp.

7

We can use some of the Thorsen money, so go along with her.'

'I just call on her, listen, say amen to everything. Right?' Glenda nodded.

'That's it. Then report to me.'

Her telephone began to ring, so I picked up the slip of paper and returned to my office.

'We have a job, Bill,' I said. 'Mrs Henry Thorsen wants an operator. I want you to go to the *Herald*'s morgue and dig out all you can about the Thorsens. I'm seeing the old trout at twelve. We'll meet here around four o'clock. Have information for me.'

Bill bounced out of his chair. This was the kind of job he liked.

'See you,' he said, and took off.

I arrived at the Thorsens' residence three minutes before twelve.

The imposing-looking house was set in two acres of woodland and lawns with a drive up to a tarmac for parking. It was one of the few houses that really had seclusion.

The house looked as if it had at least fifteen bedrooms and spacious living-rooms with terraces.

I climbed steps to the front entrance with double doors and a hanging chain bell which I tugged.

I had a five-minute wait before one of the doors opened cautiously, and I was confronted by a tall black man wearing a white coat, a black bow tie and black trousers. He was at a guess close on seventy years of age. His woolly white hair was receding.

I saw by his bloodshot eyes and the sagging muscles of his face that he was a bottle-hitter. I haven't been a private eye for more than twenty years without recognizing the signs.

'Dirk Wallace,' I said. 'Mrs Thorsen is expecting me. The Acme Detective Agency.'

He inclined his head in agreement and stood aside.

'This way, sir,' he said, and with an attempt at dignity,

but with lurching steps, he led me through a big lobby and to a door which he opened. 'Madam will be here soon,' he said, and waved me into a vast room furnished with antiques and some massive pictures, and with as much comfort as a waiting-room in a railroad station.

I moved to the big window and regarded the vast stretch of closely cut lawn and the trees, and in the distance the grey, sullen, rain-swollen clouds.

I wondered how long this drunken butler would take to tell Mrs Thorsen I had arrived.

It took twenty-five minutes by my watch. By that time I had sized up the oil paintings, priced the antique furniture and become generally bored. Then the door opened and Mrs Henry Thorsen swept in.

I had expected to see a fat, overdressed, elderly woman, the likes of whom you see everywhere in the city.

Mrs Henry Thorsen was tall and slim and figure-conscious with steel-grey hair, a rather gaunt face with good features, and piercing grey eyes which matched her imma-culate hair-do.

She regarded me as she closed the door. No smile. A lift of plucked eyebrows, the eyes going over me with a scrutiny that made me feel I had left my zipper undone.

'Mr Wallace?' Her voice was harsh and cold.

'That's correct,' I said.

She waved to a chair.

'Sit down. This need not keep me long.'

The atmosphere was every bit as warm and friendly as a funeral.

Glenda had warned me to treat this woman with kid gloves, so, with a little bow, I took the hellishly uncomfort-able chair she had indicated.

Then she proceeded to move around the room, adjusting one expensive looking knick-knack after another. From behind, she had a figure of a woman half her age. I guessed she was around 56, maybe more, but she had certainly taken care of her body.

9

I waited. I am good at waiting. Waiting is part of an operator's business.

She had reached the far end of the room, turned and paused, and again regarded me. I met her steady scrutiny with one of my own.

Although we were now some thirty feet apart, her cold, harsh voice reached me.

'I have been told your agency is the best on the east coast,' she said.

'I wouldn't be working for it if it wasn't, Mrs Thorsen,' I said.

She began to walk towards me. Her movements flowed like gentle water.

'Then I suppose, Mr Wallace, you consider yourself a good operator.'

The sneer in her voice irritated me.

'No. I don't consider myself a good operator,' I said, an edge to my voice. 'I *am* a good operator.'

She was now within six feet of me. She again stared thoughtfully at me, then nodded and sat down on one of the God-awful antique chairs that could give you a twisted spine and certainly corns on your ass.

'I have reason to believe that my daughter is being black-mailed,' she said, folding her long-fingered hands in her lap. 'I understand you people are good with cases of blackmail.'

'None better, Mrs Thorsen,' I said, my face and voice dead-pan.

'I want you to find out why my daughter is being blackmailed and who the blackmailer is.'

'With your co-operation, this should be no problem,' I said. 'Will you tell me what reasons you have to think your daughter is being blackmailed?'

'My daughter is drawing ten thousand dollars a month in cash from her account. This has become a regular with-drawal for the past ten months.' She frowned down at her hands. 'Mr Ackland has become worried, and was good enough to alert me.'

'Mr Ackland?'

'He is the family's banker: the Pacific and National. He and my late husband were very close friends.'

'Your daughter has an income of her own and her own account?'

'Unfortunately, yes. My late husband was fond of Angela, our daughter. He left her a large sum of money in trust. The monthly income from this trust is fifteen thousand. This is, of course, an absurd amount of money for a girl of her age.'

'How old is she?'

'Twenty-four.'

'I shouldn't have thought it abnormal for a girl of 24, with an income of fifteen thousand a month, to spend ten thousand a month, but you will be able to enlighten me.'

'It is certainly abnormal,' Mrs Thorsen said sharply. 'I must tell you that Angela is not a normal girl. Unfortunately, she was a measles-baby.' She paused to stare at me with those probing grey eyes. 'You understand?'

'Sure. It happens. The mother, when pregnant, catches measles, and it affects the baby.'

'Exactly. Angela is greatly retarded. She had to have a tutor, but even then, she has scarcely any education. It wasn't until she was twenty years of age that she showed signs of growing up. My husband made this absurd provision for her. For the first two months she showed no interest in the monthly income, then she began drawing these big sums every month. Mr Ackland, who is a dear friend of mine, became uneasy, and only last week he decided to consult me. He suggested to me that Angela was being blackmailed. He is very astute. I rely on him.'

'To get the record straight, Mrs Thorsen, I understand Mr Thorsen died twelve months ago. Your daughter then came into this income, and has been drawing ten thousand dollars a month for the past ten months. Is that correct?'

'Yes.'

'But for the first two months she didn't use the money?'

11

'According to Mr Ackland she spent two thousand a month to keep herself and pay the black woman who looks after her.'

'Your daughter lives with you?'

Mrs Thorsen stiffened.

'Certainly not! We are not close. As well as this absurd trust, my husband left her a cottage at the far end of the estate. She lives there with a black woman who does all the housework and provides meals. I haven't seen Angela for some weeks. She wouldn't mix with my social circle. Unfortunately, she is not attractive. She is a hopeless conversationalist.'

'Does she have friends of her own?'

'I have no idea. She lives her life, I live mine.'

'Would there be boy-friends? Maybe a special boy-friend?'

Mrs Thorsen looked sour.

'Most unlikely. I can't imagine any decent boy being interested in Angela. As I have said, she is unattractive.'

'But she is rich, Mrs Thorsen,' I pointed out. 'Lots of men can put up with unattractive girls if they have money.'

'Both Mr Ackland and I have thought of that. That is for you to find out.'

'That I can certainly do,' I said. 'I would like to know a little more about your daughter. Have you any idea how she passes her time: does she swim, play tennis, go dancing?'

Mrs Thorsen shrugged impatiently.

'I wouldn't know. As I told you we seldom meet.'

I began to dislike this woman: as a mother she wouldn't get my nomination for an Oscar.

'She is the only child?'

Mrs Thorsen stiffened, and her eyes flashed.

'I had a son, but we need not discuss him. All it is necessary to say about him is that he left home some time ago. I am glad to say I haven't seen him nor heard from him since he left. He certainly doesn't come into this problem I have with Angela.'

12

'Would you have any objection to my seeing Mr Ackland?'

'None at all. Mr Ackland has my complete confidence. In fact, it was he who suggested I should seek your help. See him by all means.'

'How about your daughter? I would have to see her.'

'Yes. Tomorrow is the first of the month. She is certain to go to the bank. Mr Ackland will arrange for you to see her, but on no account are you to approach her or speak to her. I don't want Angela to know that she is being investigated, nor do I want anyone, except Mr Ackland, to know either. I understand your agency is most discreet.'

'You can be sure of that, Mrs Thorsen.' I got to my feet. 'I will see Mr Ackland this afternoon. When I have something to tell you, I will contact you.'

'I trust you won't take long. I find your charges excessive.'

'We have a lot of work on hand, Mrs Thorsen. You can be sure we will be as quick as we can to give you the information you want.'

'When you have this information, kindly telephone for an appointment. I lead a very busy life.' She waved to the door. 'Will you see yourself out? Smedley, my butler, is a drunkard, and I disturb him as little as possible.'

'Are you thinking of getting rid of him, Mrs Thorsen?' I asked at the door.

She lifted her eyebrows and gave me a cold stare.

'Smedley has been with the family for over thirty years. He knows my habits, and is good with the silver. He also amuses my friends. Until his condition worsens, I will keep him. Goodday, Mr Wallace.'

I let myself out of the silent house, closing the front door behind me, then ran through the steady rain to my car.

After a hamburger lunch, I drove to the Pacific & National Bank, arriving there at 15.00.

The bank couldn't be faulted. It looked rich: it had two

13

alert-looking security guards, the tellers were behind bullet-proof glass. There were vases of flowers and a heavy pile carpet. The air-conditioner hummed softly.

Under the cold scrutiny of the two guards, I crossed to a desk which carried a banner: RECEPTION. Sitting behind the desk was an elderly, prune-faced woman who regarded me without enthusiasm. I could see by her expression that she had been trained to smell money, and there was no smell of money coming from me.

'Yes?'

'Mr Ackland,' I said.

'You have an appointment?'

I took from my wallet one of my professional cards and laid it before her.

'Give him this and he'll see me.'

The woman regarded the card, then stared at me.

'Mr Ackland is busy. What is your business?'

'If you are that curious,' I said, 'telephone Mrs Henry Thorsen who will explain everything to you, but, on the other hand, she might make your future life disagreeable.' I gave her my wide, friendly smile. 'Take a chance: telephone her.'

Mrs Henry Thorsen's name appeared to ring an alarm bell in her mind. She picked up my card, got to her feet and walked away, her head held high, her back rigid.

One of the security guards moved a little closer. I winked at him, and he immediately shifted his stare, fingered the butt of his gun, then moved away.

Minutes ticked by while I watched the elderly rich pay in money or draw out money and talk to the tellers who gushed, bowed and did everything servile except stand on their heads.

Prune-face returned.

'Mr Ackland will see you.' Her voice was frosty enough to put the air-conditioner on the blink. 'Over there. First door on your right.'

'Thanks,' I said and, leaving her, took her directions to

14

come up before a polished oak door with: *Horace Ackland. General Manager* printed in large gold lettering: an impressive sight. I rapped, turned the glittering brass door handle and entered an imposing office with lounging chairs, a settee, a cocktail cabinet, and a desk large enough to play snooker on.

Behind this desk sat Horace Ackland. He rose to his feet as I entered and closed the door. He was fat, short, balding and benign-looking, but there was nothing benign in his alert, brown eyes. He regarded me with a stare that could compete with a laser ray, then waved me to a chair.

'Mrs Thorsen told me you would be calling, Mr Wallace,' he said. His voice was unexpectedly deep. 'You will have some questions to ask.'

I settled myself in the comfortable chair, facing his desk while he lowered his bulk back into his chair.

'Would you give me your opinion about the daughter, Mr Ackland? Her mother says she is retarded. What do you think?'

'Frankly, I don't know. It would seem she has grown out of her handicap.' Ackland paused, then went on. 'She appears to be normal, but then I only see her for a few minutes when she picks up this money. She dresses oddly, but so do most young people. I wouldn't care to give you an opinion.'

'I understand there is a trust and she can only touch the income, which is fifteen thousand a month. What happens in the event that the daughter dies?'

His eyebrows lifted.

'She is only 24, Mr Wallace.'

'You can die by accident at any age.'

'If she dies, the trust ceases to exist, and the money goes back to the estate.'

'How much money?'

'Mr Thorsen was one of the richest men in the world. I couldn't possibly tell you how much money.'

'Mrs Thorsen has inherited his money, and at the death of her daughter, she will come into more money?'

'Yes. There are no other heirs.'

'There is a son.'

Ackland grimaced.

'Yes, Terrance Thorsen. He was disinherited when he left the Thorsen residence two years ago. He has no claim on the estate.'

'No one else?'

Ackland moved in his chair as if my questions were beginning to bore him.

'A number of bequests. Mr Thorsen left money to his butler, Smedley. The will provided Smedley with an immediate payment of five thousand dollars at Mr Thorsen's death.'

'You think, Mr Ackland, that these monthly withdrawals of ten thousand a month point to blackmail?'

Ackland placed his fingertips together, making an arch. He looked suddenly like a bishop.

'Mr Wallace, I have had thirty-five years in banking. Miss Thorsen is 24 years of age and appears, anyway to me, normal. She has the right to do what she likes with her money. But Henry Thorsen and I were very close friends, and trusted each other, and I gave him my promise that if anything should happen to him, I would keep a close eye on Angela when she inherited this fortune. Also, Mrs Thorsen is now a dear friend of mine and relies on me for financial advice, and for help in any problems which might arise. But for these special circumstances I would not have told her about these odd withdrawals. I hesitated, I admit, as it was not entirely ethical for me to tell her what Angela was doing. I held back for ten months, but as these withdrawals continued, I felt it my duty to these old friends to alert Mrs Thorsen and advise her that this possibility of blackmail should be investigated.'

'I see your point, Mr Ackland.'

'What I have told you is in strict confidence. That is understood?'

'Of course. Now, Mr Ackland, I need to know Miss

Thorsen by sight. Her mother told me on no account should I approach the girl. How do I see her?'

'Nothing easier. Tomorrow, she will arrive here to collect the money. I will arrange that you see her enter my office and leave. Then it is up to you.'

'That's fine. What time should I be here?'

'She always comes at ten o'clock. I suggest you come here at 9.45, and wait in the lobby. I will tell Miss Kertch to give you a signal when she arrives.'

A soft buzzer sounded on his desk. He lost his benign expression and looked what I knew he must be, a shrewd, tough banker.

He picked up the receiver, nodded, then said, 'In three minutes, Miss Kertch.' He looked at me. 'I'm sorry, Mr Wallace, I can give you no further time. If there is anything . . .'

I got to my feet.

'Maybe I'll need to talk to you again, Mr Ackland. I won't hold you up. I'll be here at 9.45 tomorrow.'

'Do that.' He rose to his feet and offered a firm but damp hand. 'I am sure you will be able to unravel this little problem. I have heard great things about your agency.'

Tomorrow morning should be interesting, I thought, as I got in my car. I itched to set eyes on Angela Thorsen.

Glenda Kerry heard me out, making occasional notes, as I gave her my report.

'Mrs Thorsen wants this wrapped up fast,' I concluded. 'She thinks our charges are excessive.'

'They all do, but they still come to us,' Glenda said with a wintry smile. 'What's your next move?'

'Go to the bank, tail Angela, see where she delivers the money, and with luck, get the general photo. I've got Bill digging into Thorsen's background.'

She nodded.

'OK. Go to it,' and reached for the telephone.

I found Bill at his typewriter and gave him a blow-by-blow account of my interview with Mrs Thorsen, and also with Horace Ackland.

'That's it so far,' I concluded. 'What puzzles me is why Mrs Thorsen, who couldn't care less about her daughter, who in turn couldn't care less about her, should spend good money hiring us to find out if her daughter is being blackmailed. Why? That's what I need to know. There's a smell about this that bothers me.'

'Is that our funeral, Dirk?' Bill asked. 'We have been hired to find out if and why the girl is being blackmailed. The why and the wherefore of Mrs Thorsen's motives don't concern us.'

'I think it could make this case very interesting. I can't wait to see Angela. We have to play this smooth, Bill. I'll go to the bank, wait for Ackland's signal. You will wait outside. I'll give the high sign, and you follow her from in front. We'll both have cars. She is certain to be on wheels. We mustn't lose her. She could lead us to the blackmailer.'

'OK, Dirk. Could be that easy.'

'Now, give me your report.'

'This could also be interesting. I spent the morning going through the *Herald*'s clippings on Thorsen. Make no mistake about this, Thorsen was a big wheel. He was the senior partner of Thorsen & Charteris, the top stockbrokers in this city. They have a branch in New York, but their main business is with the super-rich in this city. Thorsen had a magic touch to pick the right stock or bond, when to buy and when to sell. He not only did big deals for his clients, but also for himself.

'At the age of 35, already established as an up-and-coming broker, he married Kathleen Livingston whose father was Joe Livingston. Joe dabbled in oil, and just after the wedding, went bust on three dry wells. It was a lucky break for Kathleen to have hooked Thorsen as her family soon weren't worth a dime. There were two children: Terrance and Angela. The clippings have nothing of interest to say about them, but plenty to say of the way Mrs

Thorsen entertained and spent her husband's money. She is regarded even now as one of the big social hostesses. People flock to her parties and generally scrounge on her.

'Last year, at the age of 62, Thorsen was found dead in his library. He had a long history of heart attacks for which his doctor had treated him for some ten years. He had always lived at high pressure, making and nursing fortunes for himself and for some very influential folk in this city. It was no surprise to Mrs Thorsen or his doctor, and the death certificate was clear. Only thing the coroner, Herbert Dawson, showed interest in was how the deceased had managed to get a nasty wound on the temple, but the medical view was quite emphatic that this happened after his heart attack, when he fell and hit his head on a corner of his desk. His butler, long-serving Josh Smedley, testified that he heard a noise like a heavy fall, and hurried in, to find his master dead. He tested the breathing with a hand-mirror from the desk. Death from natural causes, and sympathy for widow and family from Coroner Herbert Dawson, who it seems is a very good friend of Mrs Thorsen's. She comes in to the money, to boost her entertaining funds, Miss Angela gets ten thousand a year, Mr Terrance gets nothing.'

'Good enough, Bill,' I said. 'It's interesting.' I thought, then took my feet off my desk. 'As you say, it's not our business to do anything except find out if Angela is being blackmailed. All the same, I am interested in the Thorsens' background. I wonder about the son, Terrance. I wonder also about the drunken butler. Well, let's make a start and open a file. You know the colonel. When he returns he'll want all the dope.'

'I guess.' Bill sighed and pulled his typewriter towards him.

It was close on 18.30 by the time we had finished and my mind was now turning to Suzy Long. This was the night when we always met at the Lobster & Crab restaurant, on the beach, among dozens of other such restaurants, but this one was reasonable in price, and the owner, Freddy Cortel, knew more about lobsters and crabs than the fishermen who caught them.

'What are you doing tonight, Bill?' I asked as I cleared my desk.

He shrugged.

'I guess I'll go back to my pad, heat up a quick-dinner mess, then watch the box until bedtime.'

Feeling a little smug, I shook my head.

'That's not the way to live, Bill. You should find yourself a nice, willing girl as I have.'

He grinned.

'Think of the money I save. Suits me. See you, Dirk,' and with a wave of his hand he took off.

I drove to my two-room apartment just on the fringe of Seacomb which is the slum district where the workers live. I parked my car and climbed up four floors in a creaking elevator to my home.

When I had first arrived in Paradise City, I found this furnished apartment going cheap, and decided it was good enough, although rather a dismal affair.

The walls were painted dark brown: the furniture was shabby and uncomfortable. The bed creaked and the mattress had lumps.

I had told myself that I wouldn't be spending much time in the place, and as the rent was so low it made sense to take it.

All that changed when Suzy insisted on visiting me. She had taken one horrified look around and exclaimed, 'You can't live in a hole like this!'

I told her about the rent and she was duly impressed.

'Right,' she said. 'Leave this to me.'

Within a week, while I stayed with Bill in his tiny pad, with the aid of two of the Bellevue Hotel painters, plus furniture from the hotel storeroom at a give-away price, Suzy converted my home into something lush. I loved it! Suzy purred every time she came in.

As you enter the apartment, you are faced with a large

20

blank wall. Neither of us had as yet decided what to do with this wall. I thought of book-shelves, but Suzy was all for finding a good copy of a modern painting. We spent much agreeable time arguing about this, and I was getting the feeling she was going to get her way.

As I entered the apartment, I was no longer confronted by the blank wall.

Instead, scrawled in aerosol black paint in six-inch letters was the message:

KEEP AWAY FROM ANGIE OR ELSE.

He must have been waiting for me behind the front door. He was quick and very expert. I just heard the swish of a descending sap, then saw flashes of light, then there was a complete blackout.

2

At 09.45 the following morning I walked, somewhat flat-footed, into the lobby of the Pacific & National Bank to be greeted with a cold stare from Miss Kertch, the receptionist.

'I will inform Mr Ackland,' she said. 'It is Mr Wallace?'

I was bored with this old trout.

'Very efficient of you, Miss Kertch. It is Miss Kertch, isn't it?'

Tight-lipped, she flicked down a switch.

'Mr Wallace is here, Mr Ackland.'

Horace Ackland, looking this time like a bishop who has breakfasted well, appeared from his office and shook hands.

'If you will sit over there, Mr Wallace, I have told Miss Kertch to alert you when Miss Thorsen arrives.'

I did just that and was glad to sink into a comfortable chair within ten feet of the reception desk.

I was battling with a life-sized headache which, in spite of Suzy's administrations and five Aspros taken this morning, still plagued me.

I thought back on the previous evening.

When Suzy arrived to pick me up, she had found the front door open, the graffiti on the wall, and me dragging myself off the floor.

Suzy was one of the rare, unflappable girls who could handle any emergency. She helped me to the settee, saw the egg-sized swelling at the back of my right ear and, without talking, dashed into the kitchen, made an ice pack and held it tenderly against the swelling. After ten minutes of this treatment, my head began to clear, and I managed a wry grin.

'Sorry about this love,' I said. 'I had an unexpected visitor.'

'Just relax, darling. Don't talk. You must get into bed.'

22

This seemed to me a good idea. With her help I undressed, crawled into my pyjamas and got into bed.

'I think a double Scotch and ice would now meet the bill,' I said as I rested my aching head on the pillow.

'No alcohol,' Suzy said firmly. 'You could have concussion. I'll call a doctor.'

'It's OK. No doctor. I've just had a professional tap on my skull. I'll be fine tomorrow. Just get me a drink.'

She sighed and left me and I heard her mixing the drink. When she returned, I was feeling better. I was glad to see she had made a drink for herself. She sat on the bed beside me and regarded me anxiously.

'It's OK, baby,' I said. 'Don't look so tragic.'

She took a long pull at her drink and shivered.

'You scared the life out of me. Oh, Dirk, what's been happening?'

'Nothing for you to worry your pretty head about. I'm working on a new case. It would seem I have opposition.'

'Oh.' Suzy nodded. By now, she knew that I never talked about my work. I had drummed into her head that no Acme operator was allowed to talk about his case. 'I can't ask who Angie is?'

'You can't ask – period.'

'Right. I'm going to give you three sleeping-pills and I'm going to leave you to sleep.' She went into the bathroom, found the pills and returned. 'Now be good, Dirk. You need a long sleep.'

'I could do with your company in bed.'

'No way. Take these pills.'

By the way my head was splitting open, it wasn't such a bad idea, so I took them.

'I'll get my painter pals in tomorrow to fix that wall. How did these people get in?'

'I guess they picked the lock.'

'Right. I'll get a locksmith here tomorrow to really fix your door. I'll put the new keys in your mailbox.' She bent and kissed me. 'Now, sleep,' and she left me.

I did sleep, and although I still had a bad headache, I had met Bill outside his apartment block at 09.15. He in his car and I in mine, we drove to the bank. As we were early, I sat in his car and filled him in about the previous night. He listened, nodding from time to time.

'Looks like trouble, Dirk,' he said.

'Feels like it, too. But trouble is our business.'

'Quick work, huh? Someone must have alerted these guys that you were investigating Angie. They went into action fast. Who alerted them?'

'That's something we have to find out.'

It was now close on 09.45. I slid out of his car.

'I'll give you the high sign,' I said and walked into the lobby of the bank.

At least it had stopped raining. I sat in the comfortable chair, pretending to read *The Paradise City Herald*, and keeping one eye on Miss Kertch who was busy answering the telephone in a low, inaudible voice, pressing buttons and looking sour.

Then suddenly, she rose to her feet and produced an autumnal smile, a few degrees less chilly than her wintry smile.

I guessed the big moment had arrived. I looked towards the bank's entrance.

A girl had entered and was saluted by the doorman. She came across the big lobby swiftly. I had time to give her an in-depth look.

Thin as a matchstick: no front, no behind, she wore a big straw hat like those you see on the heads of peons working in the fields in Mexico. The hat was pulled down, obscuring her face. She wore four-inch sun-goggles. Her clothes were a dark loosely fitting T-shirt, and the usual blue jeans every girl, all over the world, wears. She had on sandals. Her toe-nails weren't painted. She could pass as any young girl tourist on vacation. As heiress to the Thorsens' billions, she couldn't have been more incognito than Garbo in her prime.

Miss Kertch was already leading her to Ackland's office.

24

I hurried out to where Bill was sitting in his car.

'The chick in the straw hat and jeans,' I said. 'You spotted her?'

'I guessed she was our party,' Bill said. 'That's her car, two cars ahead. A Volkswagen. She's certainly keeping a low profile.'

'OK, Bill. I'll leave my car,' and I slid in beside him. 'We'll wait and follow her.'

She appeared some ten minutes later. She had with her a small plastic brief-case, no doubt supplied by Ackland, and no doubt containing ten thousand dollars in big bills.

There was no problem following her. She drove at the correct speed, then turned off the boulevard and headed towards the waterfront. She then turned left, heading away from the harbour where the rich anchored their yachts, turned down another side-street and got onto the waterfront where the fishing boats were anchored and the riff-raff lived.

At this hour there was some activity. The fishermen were coming from the bars to board their vessels for a second morning's catch. The young hippies were drinking coffee, gaping with sleep. Angela parked in an empty slot and Bill drove by her, swung the Olds into another parking slot and cut the engine.

I got out of the car in time to see her walk across the waterfront, dodging the heavy trucks and heading towards a row of bars, cafés and sleazy restaurants. I watched her enter a broken-down-looking dump with *The Black Cassette: Disco. Drinks. Quick Eats* printed across the facia in peeling black lettering.

Moving slowly, I crossed the waterfront and paused outside the finger-stained glass door. There was a notice pasted on the door:

COLOURED BRETHREN ONLY:
WHITE FOLK NOT ADMITTED:
HEAR?

After hesitating, I decided it was too soon to stick my nose into what could be a hornet's nest. I needed information. I returned to the car where Bill was waiting.

'Strictly for blacks,' I said. 'You wait here. See how long she remains in the joint. I'm going to dig for info.'

I made my way along the crowded waterfront and arrived outside the Neptune Tavern where I was sure I would find Al Barney. Like a permanent fixture, he was sitting on a bollard, twiddling an empty beer can in his hand while he stared gloomily out to sea.

Al Barney was known as the doyen of the waterfront. He claimed, and rightly, that he was a man with his ear to the ground. There was little he didn't know about the waterfront's machinations.

Balding, wearing a dirty sweat-shirt and duck frayed trousers, he supported an enormous beer belly on his knees. Apart from collecting information, Barney's main interest was beer and sausages dipped in some horribly potent sauce that would skin the mouth of any ordinary man, but on which Barney doted.

He and the Acme Agency often got together: the operators supplying him with beer, and he providing the operators with useful information.

When he saw me he gave me his shark-like smile and tossed the empty beer can into the sea.

'Glad to see you, Mr Wallace,' he said, 'very glad. I was just thinking it was time for breakfast.' He peered thoughtfully at me. 'You feel like breakfast?'

'Let's go to the Neptune,' I said. 'I'll buy you beer and breakfast.'

'Spoken like the gent you are,' Barney said. He heaved his bulk off the bollard and waddled across the waterfront to the Neptune Tavern. I followed him.

Once inside the dingy, dark bar room, Barney waved to Sam, the black barkeeper.

'Breakfast, Sam,' Barney said, 'and let's have some action.'

'Yes, Mr Barney, sir,' Sam said, giving me a wide, flashing smile. 'And Mr Wallace? You like a coffee or something?'

Having tried Sam's coffee, which was terrible, I shook my head.

'Later, perhaps, Sam. I've just had breakfast.'

Barney was already seated at his favourite table in a corner. I joined him.

'How are things with you, Mr Wallace?' he asked. 'OK? You look fine. Is the colonel OK?'

I knew the ritual well by now. Barney must never be rushed. He must never be asked questions until his third beer, and only when he had finished a plate of the deadly sausages.

'The colonel right now is in Washington,' I said, lighting a cigarette. 'I'm fine. And you, Al?'

'Well, I guess I'm not getting any younger. But who is?' Barney shook his balding head. 'But I'm not grumbling. The tourist trade is starting next month.' His little eyes lit up. 'Marvellous people – tourists. They come and talk to me, take my photograph. I tell them things that make them pee in their pants.' He gave his shark-like grin. 'I guess everyone likes to hear scandal.'

Sam came across and planted down a pint of beer and a big dish of the most dreadful-looking little sausages that only the devil could have invented. Barney promptly threw three into his mouth, chewed, gulped, and tears rose to his eyes. He swallowed, gasped and drank half the beer.

'You don't know what you're missing, Mr Wallace. Nothing like them. Try one.'

'No, thank you.'

He threw three more into his mouth and went through the same performance.

'Wonderful for the digestion.' He finished the beer and Sam slid across to place a refill.

I waited patiently.

Finally, the sausages and yet another beer finished, Barney released a belch that made the windows rattle.

'Now, what can I do for you, Mr Wallace?' he asked with his shark-like smile.

'What can you tell me about the Black Cassette?'

Barney lifted what eyebrows he had left.

'A black hang-out. Dancing, poor grub, but popular.'

I waited, looking directly at him.

'No cop trouble,' Barney went on. 'The joint was bought by a black about a year ago. He made it into a sort of club. We don't have a lot of blacks here: most are Vietnamese and Ricans. This joint is a place where the blacks can get together, feel at home, dance.'

'Who bought the place, Al?'

Barney scratched his throat. It was a sign I had learned to know so I signalled to Sam who came sliding across the room with another beer.

'These little lovies give a man a thirst,' Barney said. 'You're a swell, Mr Wallace.'

'Who bought the place?' I repeated.

Barney took a long pull at his beer glass.

'A no-good black,' he said, scowling. 'How he got the money to buy the joint surprised me. Five thousand bucks for a ten-year lease. My guess is he must have got the money from his pa who used to be a drinking friend of mine. A nice old guy. He'd come down here and talk with me and buy me beer.' Barney shook his head and looked sad. 'Then a year ago, I didn't see him any more. An old guy like me misses good friends.'

'What's the name of this new owner?' I asked.

'Him? Hank Smedley. You don't want to have anything to do with him, Mr Wallace. He's tough and nasty, and doesn't dig interference.'

I kept my face expressionless.

'The name of his father?'

'Josh Smedley. He works as the butler to that rich, snooty bitch, Mrs Henry Thorsen. From what I hear, poor old

Josh is now hitting the bottle. I don't blame him. What with his no-good son, his wife quitting him and Mrs T., it's enough to drive any guy to the bottle.'

'His wife left him?'

Barney nodded and took another gulp of beer.

'That's right, Mr Wallace. He told me about it. The trouble there was Mrs Smedley just couldn't put up with her son. He was and is a wild one, but poor Josh loved him. He and his wife were always fighting over Hank. Finally, when Mr Thorsen died, they split. Josh looked after Mrs T. and Hanna – the wife – looked after the daughter who came into a load of money left her by her father.' Barney sighed. 'The way the rich live! Still, I don't envy them. What with taxes, their children and divorces: not for me. I like the life I live. I've no problems.'

'Good for you. Know anything about the daughter, Al?'

'Can't say I do. I heard she was a nut-case. I did hear that when she was around 16 or so, Hank was screwing her. Don't quote me, Mr Wallace. This was just a rumour. She could be one of the girls who like to be screwed.' Barney shook his head. 'This is the modern thing. It was different when I was a kid. Then I really had to work for it.' A sudden crafty look came into his eyes. 'You interested in Angie Thorsen, Mr Wallace?'

'More interested in Hank Smedley.'

'Well, Mr Wallace, be careful how you tread with that one. He's dangerous: wild and vicious.'

'Angie had a brother: Terrance. Know anything about him?'

Barney looked down at his empty plate, then thoughtfully at me. I took the hint.

'Go ahead, Al,' I said.

'This is my breakfast and my lunch,' Barney said, and gave an elaborate signal to Sam who rushed over with another plate-load of sausages and a pint of beer. 'A man of my size has to keep his strength up.' He popped three of the sausages into his mouth, chewed, grunted

29

and nodded his approval. 'What were you asking, Mr Wallace?'

'Do you know anything about Terrance Thorsen?'

'You could say I know something. He and his pa didn't get along. Terry walked out and got a room on the waterfront. A sleazy old condo called Breakers, you wouldn't want to know it. This would be some two years ago. He played a hot piano, so I've been told. I never heard him. He got taken on at the Dead-End Club which is run by Harry Rich. The boy changed his name to Terry Zeigler. I heard he increased the club's business no end. The swinging kids were crazy about his playing. He played every night, nine till two, never spoke to anyone. Just played. Then around three months ago, he dropped out of sight. No one has seen him around since then, though I did sort of hear that this Hank poison tried to poach him away, but it would have been hot news if Zeigler had played at the Black Cassette, and that's never happened. No sir. Not likely.'

I thought it was time to go. I didn't want Barney to know how much I needed information. I took out my wallet and produced a twenty bill which I slid over to him.

'Keep your ear to the ground. Hank, Terry and even Angie. OK?'

He gave me his shark-like smile and snapped up the bill the way a lizard snaps up a fly.

'You know how to find me, Mr Wallace. I'll listen.'

'See you, Al.'

I crossed over to Sam, paid the check, then walked out into the steamy humid atmosphere.

I felt my morning wasn't wasted.

I found Bill, sitting in the car, chewing gum and mopping the sweat off the back of his neck.

I slid in beside him.

'She shown yet?'

'Ten minutes ago. I didn't know if I should follow her

30

or wait for you. She wasn't carrying the plastic bag, and she took off up-town.'

'OK. I've a raft of information.' I told him what I had learned from Barney.

'So we have to go some place – after we've had a beer?'

'Next stop the Breakers,' I said. 'Before beer.'

'I guessed that,' Bill said, and began to mop his face.

We found the Breakers condo down a side-street. It was a typical dwelling that housed the many workers that went daily to the city to pander to the rich: shabby, with paint peeling, surrounded by small shops that sold anything from fish to pantihose.

The narrow street was crowded with Vietnamese, Ricans, a few blacks, and white elderly women with shopping bags.

Bill found parking space with a struggle, and we walked back to the entrance of the condo.

'Wait around, Bill. I'll go talk to the janitor.'

I found the janitor on the basement floor. He was using a broom as if his hands were tender. He was a big, fat, hairy lump of a man, wearing a dirty singlet and dirtier trousers. He leaned on his broom and regarded me.

'I am looking for Terry Zeigler,' I said, giving him my cop stare.

'OK.' He nodded. 'You look for him. I've got work to do.' He began sweeping again.

'Where do I find him?'

He paused, stared at me, then asked, 'You a cop?'

'I'm looking for him because he has come into some money.'

He stopped his tender sweeping and interest suddenly lit up his face which looked as if a child had carved out his features from a lump of lard.

'Much?'

'I don't know. No one tells me anything.'

It's wonderful how this worn-out gag works, I thought.

'Would there be a reward?'

'Could be twenty bucks if I was steered right.'

31

He scratched his hairy arm while he thought, then leant his massive weight on the broom handle.

'Terry Zeigler?'

'Right.'

'He rented the top apartment around eighteen months ago. Paid steadily. No problems, though he seemed to work night and days. Then two months ago, he took off. He told me he was quitting, paid the rent, slung a couple of suitcases in that Olds of his and left. That's the last I've seen of him.'

Patiently, I asked, 'He didn't say where he was going?'

'No. Why should I care? They come and they go.'

'An Olds, you say. Remember the number?'

This large lump of fat seemed to me as helpful as a fractured leg, but this one registered, even brought a gleam of intelligence to the lardy face.

'Sure I remember a simple number like that. Want to write it down? PC10001.'

'Did someone take his apartment?'

'Yeah. Zeigler hadn't been gone more than an hour when this girl arrived. She paid two months' rent in advance, and moved in.'

'Who is she?'

'Dolly Gilbert. Anyway, that's what she calls herself. I know nothing about her. She works nights is all.'

He began to move his broom restlessly so I decided maybe a little oil might produce something more tangible. I took out my wallet, thumbed out a five-dollar bill and let him see it.

He eyed the bill and stopped his sweeping.

'That for me?'

'Could be if you are more helpful. I have to find Zeigler. Surely someone in this building can give me a lead.'

'Yeah.' He paused to scratch his arm. I could almost hear his brains creak while he thought. 'Come to think of it your best bet would have been Miss Angus. She could have told you about Zeigler. She lived in the apartment opposite his.

She was a nice old lady: shoving 80. She cleaned for him and gave him a hot meal from time to time. She was one of these old girls who like being helpful. Nothing she liked better than to yak with people. She yakked with me until I nearly blew my top. Yeah, I guess, she could have told you about Zeigler.'

'Could have?' I asked. 'Has she left?'

The janitor made restless movements, his eyes on the five-dollar bill so I gave it to him. He regarded the bill, kissed it and stowed it away in a pocket of his dirty trousers.

'She certainly left – feet first. That was three days after Zeigler quit.'

'What do you mean – feet first?'

'When I was cleaning up on Miss Angus's floor, I saw her front door was ajar. I remembered I hadn't seen her for a couple of days, so I looked in. There was Miss Angus lying on the floor. She was dead. I called the cops, and left it to them.' He again scratched his arm. 'I can do without the fuzz asking questions and making pests of themselves. I couldn't tell them a thing. Finally the cops decided it was some junkie, looking for money, who killed her. He had punched her in the face and her home was turned over. At her age, a punch in the face is a killer. I guess she could have told you where you might find Zeigler. She often spoke to me about him, saying what a nice boy he was. I shouldn't think he would have walked out of here without telling her where he was going. Well, that's it. Can't do more for you, can I?'

'Someone take on Miss Angus's apartment?'

'Not yet. She had a three-year lease and her own furniture. Some lawyer is tying up her affairs. As soon as he's finished, the apartment will go fast.'

'Do you know who the lawyer is?'

'Some Yid. He came to see me.'

'Know his name?'

The janitor scratched his arm again, thought, then said, 'Solly Lewis.'

I decided he wasn't going to produce any further information of interest.

'OK, and thanks,' I said. 'Maybe, I'll be seeing you later with another five-dollar bill.'

He nodded.

'That's fine with me. Come as often as you like.'

I climbed the stairs to the lobby and went out into the humid heat where Bill was leaning against our car, chewing gum.

'Getting places,' I said. 'Find out the address of a lawyer: Solly Lewis. I'll be back in a while.'

I returned to the lobby and took the elevator to the top floor. There were only two apartments up there. On the right-hand door was a sticker that read *Miss Dolly Gilbert*.

I leaned against the bell push. Waited, then leaned again. I thought at this hour, which was now 17.50, Dolly might just be out of bed. I had to ring a third time before the front door jerked open.

I was confronted by a girl who looked around 20 years of age: a blonde, with curly hair, a face plastered with make-up, a mouth that told me that she had lived tough, and still lived that way. She was wearing a wrap that hung open. Apart from a pair of pink panties, she was naked.

She looked me over, then smiled. Her smile was that hard, welcoming smile a whore knows how to give.

'Sorry, buster,' she said. 'In a couple of hours, huh? I've got a friend here right now.'

'So what do I do? Wait around for a couple of hours?' I said, giving her my friendly smile. 'A pal of mine told me you could take care of me.'

I was looking beyond her at the big room, comfortably furnished with ageing furniture. Across the room was a door that probably led into the bedroom. The door was half open.

'I sure can,' she said, 'but right now . . .'

A voice suddenly boomed out of the bedroom.

'Tell that fink to piss off! Let's have some action! You think I've got all the goddam day?'

34

The girl stiffened.

'Man! He sure is a wild one. See you,' and she slammed the door in my face.

I knew for sure that harsh, booming voice had come from the mouth of a negro. There was no mistaking the lilt.

'A wild one', the girl had said.

I had a hunch. I rode the elevator down and joined Bill.

'Get the address?'

'Yeah. He's in the book. 67, Seacomb Road.'

'OK. Listen, Bill, within a short while, a black will appear. I want you to stay with him. I'll leave you the car in case he's on wheels. Stay with him. I want to know if he could just be Hank Smedley.'

'And you?'

'I'm going to talk to Solly Lewis.'

Seeing a passing taxi, I flagged it down.

3

I found Solly Lewis on the top floor of a shabby block in a small room that pretended to be an office: a battered desk, a still more battered filing cabinet and a typewriter, standing on a small table that told me he did his own typing.

He was sitting behind the desk with a thin file before him. He regarded me coolly, then got to his feet. He was of average height, around 35 years of age, with thick black hair and a beard that nearly obscured his face. His clothes had done much service, and he was painfully thin as if he had only one square meal a week.

'What can I do for you?' he asked, and offered his hand.

I shook his hand, then taking out my wallet, I gave him my professional card. He waved me to the only other chair. It looked so elderly I was nervous lowering my weight onto it.

He sat down and studied my card, then looked up at me, his black eyes lighting up.

'Well, Mr Wallace, I'm glad to meet you,' he said. 'Of course, I know all about your agency. What can I do for you?'

'I understand you are acting for the late Miss Angus.'

I saw him stiffen.

'That is correct. I am her executor.'

'Does the name Terrance Thorsen or Terry Zeigler mean anything to you?'

He nodded.

'Terry Zeigler. Yes, of course.'

'I am trying to find him. As Miss Angus and he were friendly I hoped she could have told me where he is, but it seems she is unfortunately dead, so it occurred to me that you might remember her mentioning him to you.'

36

Lewis pulled at his beard as he regarded me.

'Why do you want to find him?'

'The Acme Agency has been hired to find him. I haven't been told who the client is. I've just been told to find him.'

'Then you and I seem to have the same problem,' Lewis said, relaxing in his chair. 'Miss Angus left all her money and effects to Zeigler. I can't clear up her estate until I have found Zeigler, and up to now, I have not been successful.'

'But I understand Miss Angus lived in rather a depressed state. She cleaned for Zeigler. How come she would have anything to leave him in her will?'

'Her estate is worth a hundred thousand dollars, clear of tax,' Lewis said, not hiding the wistful note in his voice. 'Miss Angus was eccentric. She never spent her money. She hoarded it. I finally convinced her she should not keep all this money in envelopes, hidden in her home, and persuaded her to put this money in a bank. I am glad to say she did this.'

'She must have been a real character. You are sure she did put the money in the bank?'

'Oh, yes. I have checked. She deposited the money with the Pacific & National Bank four days before she was murdered. I am in touch with Mr Ackland, the general manager there. It is now a matter of locating Zeigler.'

'What have you done to find him?'

He gave a weary smile.

'The usual things: advertising, the police, the Missing Person's Bureau. I have done the best I can, but, up to now, and it's two months ago, I haven't been able to trace Zeigler.' He leaned forward and looked hopefully at me. 'But now you are also looking for him, this gives me hope. If you can't find him, who can?'

'Suppose he's dead? What happens to the money?'

'If he died after Miss Angus it would go to his next of kin. But I have to be sure he is dead.'

Another blind alley.

I got back to my office by taxi. Thankful for the air-conditioner, I sat at my desk and typed my report. I had just finished when Bill came in, mopping his face.

'Hell!' he moaned, dropping into his chair. 'It's awful outside.'

'What have you got for me?'

'Good hunch of yours. A big black buck came out, got into a white Caddy and took off. I followed him to the Black Cassette. He got out and went in, then a young black came out and took the Caddy away.'

'Tell me about the big black.'

Bill grimaced.

'A real tough, and make no mistake about that. He stands around six foot six: a small head on shoulders a yard wide. He was wearing a sweat-shirt and I could see his muscles, like oranges, rippling. He moved like a dancer. He had hands like hams. He looked as dangerous as a cobra. That's it, Dirk. I didn't need to enquire if he was Hank Smedley.'

I looked at my watch. It was close on two hours since I had talked to Dolly Gilbert. It was time to see her again. I gave Bill my report.

'See you, Bill. Stick around,' and leaving him, I rode down to the street, got in my car and headed for the Breakers.

I had only to thumb her bell push when the door jerked open, and there she was, giving me the usual whore's smile of welcome.

'Come on in, gorgeous,' she said. 'Sorry about the delay, but that's the way the cookie crumbles.'

I entered the big living-room as she closed the door.

'Look, honey,' she said, 'I'm a little pressed for time. Let's have my present – fifty bucks, and let's go into action. Right?'

I walked by her into the bedroom, looked into the kitchen, then the tiny bathroom, then satisfied we were alone, I returned to the bedroom where she was standing by the bed, regarding me uneasily.

'You scared of something, mister?' she asked.

'No. I want to talk to you, Dolly.' Taking her by her arm, I led her back into the living-room. 'Sorry, baby, but this isn't your kind of business.' I gave her my professional card, then sat down in a shabby but comfortable chair.

She stared for some moments at the card, then she walked up to me and thrust the card at me. She said in a harsh voice, 'On your way, Buster! Get the hell out of here!'

'I am looking for information,' I said, giving her my friendly smile. 'It pays a hundred bucks. Now don't tell me you're not interested in a hundred bucks.'

She stared, then held out her hand.

'Let's see the money.'

I took out my wallet, found a hundred-dollar bill, showed it to her, then folded and palmed it.

'Do we talk?'

She sat down in a chair near mine. Her wrap came apart. She was naked, but her body didn't appeal to me. OK, she was slim, with good-looking breasts, a flat tummy and dark pubic hair, but she was shop-soiled: not surprising by the way she lived.

'Talk about what?'

I put my card back in my wallet.

'I'm looking for Terry Zeigler.'

Her eyes became alert.

'What makes you think I know anything about Terry?'

'I don't. I'm looking for him. I was told you moved into this pad within a couple of hours of him moving out. I thought he might have tipped you off this pad was coming vacant, and you might know where I can find him.'

'Is it straight that I get that money?' She drew in a deep breath. 'Brother! Can I use money right now!'

'Give out, and you get it. Did he tip you he was leaving?'

'No, But I heard pretty smart. I have friends here and there, though I never got along with Terry.'

To help her to become more out-giving, I unfolded the hundred-dollar bill, regarded it, then refolded it.

'You don't know where I can find Terry Zeigler?'

39

'Is he in trouble? He kinda left in a hurry. Scared maybe?'

'I'd say not. Someone has left him money, and it's my job to find him and give him the money.'

Her eyes widened.

'How much?'

'I wouldn't know. It's not peanuts.' I smiled at her. 'Do you or don't you know where I can find Terry?'

She shook her head.

'No, Buster. I don't know. Imagine that odd guy coming into money! Oh, how I wish someone would leave me some money!'

Was this going to be another dead-end, I wondered.

'What makes you say Terry is an odd guy?'

'I only met him a couple of times. He never opened his mouth. He just stared at me as if I was something he had stepped in on the sidewalk. He certainly played a hot piano. If you ask me, I guess he was either crazy or doped.'

'Do you think he's a junkie, Dolly?'

'How the hell do I know? Most of the finks around here are on the needle. That's something I leave alone. I've got to earn money.'

I leaned forward and gave her the hundred-dollar bill.

'Well, thanks. You've been helpful,' I said. 'There is one more thing. Does Hank Smedley often visit you?'

She reared back as if I had hit her, then jumped to her feet. Her face was the colour of a soiled sheet.

'Get out!' she screamed. 'I've had enough of you! Get out.'

In my twenty-odd years as an operator, I have seen frightened faces, but none so frightened as this trembling, wretched little whore. Frightened? No, rather terrified.

I left her clutching the bill, shaking; I knew there was nothing more I could get from her.

I rode down in the creaking elevator and walked to where I had parked my car.

* * *

Back in my office, I found Bill at his desk, chewing gum and re-reading my report.

I told him what I had got from Dolly.

'Look, Dirk, I'm not with you. Why the interest in Terry Thorsen? We're supposed to . . .'

'Sure,' I broke in, 'but we have no real leads. I have a hunch that Terry could put us right. I want to find him and talk to him.'

'Shouldn't we concentrate on Hank Smedley?'

'I want to find Terry first.'

He shrugged.

'Well, OK, you're the boss. So now what?'

'For you, home, and forget all this. For me, I'm adding to my report, then home and early to bed. Alone.'

'You OK, Dirk?'

'Go home!' and I waved him away.

As I opened the front door that had been fitted with two new locks, the keys to which I found in my mailbox, a smell of fresh paint greeted me. The graffiti had been painted over, and my home was back to normal.

What a girl! I thought, as I shut and locked the door. I telephoned the Bellevue Hotel only to be told that Suzy was handling an insurge of tourists and wouldn't be available for at least two hours, so I couldn't even thank her.

The following morning, I was at my desk early. I was just finishing my report when Bill came in.

'Sleep well?' he asked, but he knew better than to expect an answer.

'I want you to trace an Olds. PC10001. I want it fast, and in depth.'

'Right.'

He took off. Bill had now almost as many contacts in the city as I had, and very usefully he was a buddy with the officer in charge of car registration.

I finished my report, filed it, then went along to Glenda

41

Kerry's office. She had just come in and was going through the mail.

'Hi, Glenda!' I said. 'The Thorsen case.'

She sat back.

'What's new?'

I gave her a synopsis of what I had learned, and concluded, 'Angela Thorsen seems to be paying money to someone in this Black Cassette. Whether it is Hank Smedley or someone else, I haven't found out. I can't see a way of finding out without talking to Angela or Hank. I'm not crazy about doing that. Terry would be useful if I could find him. This case, if we're going to get a satisfactory report, could take time.'

'We are charging Mrs Thorsen three thousand a day. You had better see her, report to her, and ask her if she wants to go on. Maybe she won't. Get her reaction, Dirk.'

That made sense to me, so I returned to my office. As the time was 10.20, I phoned the Thorsens' residence.

I recognized Smedley's slurred voice.

'Mrs Thorsen, please,' I said. 'Mr Wallace.'

'The detective gentleman?' Smedley asked, after a pause.

'That is correct.'

'Mrs Thorsen is out. She won't be returning until late this afternoon.'

I thanked him, then hung up. After a couple of minutes' thought, an idea struck me. I immediately acted on it. Scribbling a note for Bill and leaving it on his desk, I went down to my car and drove to the Thorsens' residence. With Mrs Thorsen out of the way I would have the opportunity for a talk with Josh Smedley.

I had a six-minute wait and tugged the bell chain three times, before the front door opened.

'Sorry, Mr Wallace,' he muttered. 'Mrs Thorsen is out.'

'So you told me.' Using my beef, I moved forward and entered the lobby. 'I need to talk to you, Josh.'

He gave way. He had no alternative. When I was in the lobby, he reluctantly closed the front door.

42

'Excuse me, Mr Wallace, I am busy,' he said in a quavering voice.

'Let's go to your den,' I said, taking a firm grip on his arm. 'I've a few questions to ask.'

He stared at me uneasily for a few moments, then he moved down the long corridor and finally came to a good-sized room with four armchairs, a bed, closets and another door I guessed led to a bathroom. Smedley was certainly living in comparative luxury.

'Let's have a drink, Josh,' I said. 'Scotch for me.'

He hesitated, then moved to a closet, produced a bottle of Cutty Sark, poured two generous drinks into glasses and replaced the bottle. Over his shoulder, I saw a neat row of empty Cutty Sark bottles on the top shelves of the closet.

With a shaky hand he handed me one glass, then holding tightly to his glass, he lowered himself into a chair near mine.

'What do you want to know, Mr Wallace?' he asked, and as if to give himself support, he took a gulp from his glass.

'Mrs Thorsen has hired me, Josh, to find out if, why and by whom her daughter is being blackmailed. I guess you know this?'

He nodded.

'You know everything that goes on here, don't you, Josh?'

'I've worked for Mr and Mrs Thorsen for over thirty years,' he said carefully.

'I would like you to tell me what kind of man Mr Thorsen was. This is confidential, Josh, but it is important.'

'Mr Thorsen is dead.'

'I know that. What kind of man was he?'

'Mr Thorsen was a hard man,' he said, after a long pause. 'I guess he had to be to get to his position. He drove me hard, but he paid well. Yes, Mr Thorsen was a hard man.'

'He was hard on his children?'

'Mr Terry, yes, but not Miss Angela. He wanted Mr Terry to go into his business. He had no patience with Mr

Terry's piano playing. Yes. He was very hard on Mr Terry. Finally, Mr Terry walked out. I was pleased.' He gazed into space, his wrinkled face lighting up with a smile. 'It was a very unhappy place here until Mr Terry left. After that, the place was all right until Mr Thorsen died. Then there was an upset. Miss Angela and her mother didn't get on, so Miss Angela left to live in the cottage, and as my wife didn't get on with me, she went to look after Miss Angela.'

'You must have seen the two children grow up from babies,' I said. 'How did you react to Terry?'

Smedley stared gloomily at his empty glass.

'Mr Terry was a good boy, Mr Wallace. He and I got along fine together. He would often come into this room and talk with me. He was interested in my past and my parents. It made him sad that my wife and I didn't get along together. He told me he couldn't put up with his father any longer. As soon as Mr Thorsen went off to his office, Mr Terry would go up to the music room and play and play. He was a natural genius. He couldn't read music. He had only to hear a tune and he could play it. His father wouldn't allow him to take lessons, but he didn't want lessons. He just played. When he left, that was some two years ago, he came to me, took my hand and said goodbye. I was so upset, I just gripped his hand, and when he had gone, I cried.'

'That glass looks empty, Josh,' I said. 'What's wrong with a refill?'

He scrambled to his feet and lurched to the closet.

'How about you, Mr Wallace?'

'I'm fine.'

He came back to his chair, nursing another big Scotch.

'How about Miss Angela?' I asked. 'How did you get along with her?'

'When she was a kid, Mr Wallace, we go along fine, but when she began to grow up, she became difficult. She got to dislike me. I guess my wife put in the poison. No, I guess Miss Angela and me didn't get along.'

'Did she get along with her brother?'

He nodded.

'They were very close. Oh, yes. I liked to see them together. When he left home, she changed. It was as if the sun had gone out of her life. Then when Mr Thorsen died, she moved into the cottage and my wife went with her. I don't see her any more.' He drank and sighed, and I could see the sadness on his shrivelled face.

'Mr Thorsen died suddenly, a year ago?'

'Yes, but not unexpected.'

'How's that, Josh?'

'He was a strong-living man. Very – hot, fierce. Too much for his weak heart. He had been warned by his doctor many times. But he had to have his own way all the time.'

'Did that make it difficult for you?'

'Not me. I knew him, over all those years, but some people . . .'

'Some people upset him easily?'

'Surely.'

'Did he quarrel with them?'

'Not quarrelling, because he had business to do with them. He was very clever with money, those folks' money.'

'But he often lost his temper with them?'

'Yes. With them, with me, even with . . .'

'Even Miss Angie?'

'Well, just that once, about Mr Terry.'

'When was that, Josh?'

'That day . . .' He reached for another gulp at his drink.

'Did you hear them quarrelling? Miss Angie raise her voice at him?'

'I don't listen to all that. It's just voices at me. I did hear her say Mr Terry's name, quite loud. Then she went out.'

'Did you tell the coroner that?'

'He never asked, and it was family talk, purely family talk.'

'I am looking for Terry. It's important that I find him. Can you tell me where he is?'

Smedley shook his head.

'I wish I could, Mr Wallace. I would so much like to see him again and talk with him. I haven't heard from him since he walked out.'

'I'll tell you why it is important that I get in contact with him. An old lady has left him one hundred thousand dollars. She was a Miss Angus and she was murdered. The money can't come to him until I can contact him. One hundred thousand dollars, Josh.'

I waited, watching him.

'The old lady was murdered?' he asked, staring at me.

'Yes. The killer must have found out that she kept all this money in her apartment at the Breakers where Terry lived. The killer was looking for the money, but he was too late. It is now in a bank, and waiting for Terry to claim it.'

'I just don't know where he is, Mr Wallace.'

I got to my feet and moved to the door.

'Just one thing,' I said. 'You have a son, Hank, who runs the Black Cassette Disco. Correct?'

He shrivelled back in his chair.

'That is right, Mr Wallace,' he said in a low, quavering voice.

'When I first came here and Mrs Thorsen hired me, you telephoned your son, telling him about me, didn't you?'

He remained silent, closing his eyes, his drink trembling in his hand.

'Didn't you?' I barked, using my cop voice.

'I talk to my son every day,' he muttered.

'You told him about me?'

'My son is interested in what goes on here,' he said after a long pause.

'OK, Josh,' I said, not taking it further. I had the answer. Smedley had tipped his son that I had been hired to watch Angela, and Hank had immediately given me a warning, spoiling my wall, and taking it further to underline the message, had sapped me.

I let myself out and Smedley seemed hardly to notice.

* * *

46

Back in my office, I found my note to Bill still on his desk. I sat at my desk and made a report of my talk with Josh Smedley. By the time I had finished it was 13.15, and I was hungry. As I was putting my report in the Thorsen file, Bill came in. I could see by his excited expression he had news.

'Let's eat, Bill,' I said, getting to my feet.

'Great! I could eat an elephant!'

Without further talk, we went down to a restaurant that was close by, just around the corner from the Trueman building.

We ordered breaded lamp chops and french fries: the special for the day. We both had beers. The service was fast. We had scarcely time to settle ourselves when two plates arrived with two enormous lamb chops and a mountain of french fries. The lamb chops were as tender as an old man's leg, but we were hungry, so we chewed.

'What's new, Bill?' I asked as I sawed at my meat.

'The Olds is now registered in the name of Hank Smedley. Transferred to him some three months ago. How do you like that?'

'I like it,' I said and ate some of the crisp potatoes. 'And . . . ?'

'Plenty,' Bill said. 'I got Hank's address. 56, Seagrove Road, Secombe. I went along and took a look. Hank has a pad on the top floor. The place is nice and with style. I then went along to the cop house and talked to Tom Lepski. I told him we were interested in Hank Smedley. As he had nothing to do, he gave out. The cops know all about Hank. Lepski dug out his file. Hank's been in trouble since the age of twelve. D.J. Three times in a reform. Stealing, violence, beating up kids: a real hellion. Then suddenly he appears to have turned respectable. Yet Lepski said he has a hunch that something is going on there, but he doesn't know what. He itches to raid the place, but can't get a search-warrant. That's about it, Dirk.'

'Nice work,' I said.

As we chewed I told him what I had learned from Josh

Smedley, which didn't seem to add up to much, but left a doubt or two, a whiff of a scent we would have to pick up somewhere.

While Bill was thumping out his report, I read through every word in the Thorsen file. The time now was 16.15. I wondered if Mrs Thorsen was back home. No harm in trying, I thought, and taking it slow, I drove to the Thorsens' residence.

The humid drizzle had stopped and the sun had come out. I was in luck. As I walked up the drive, leaving my car parked outside the villa's gates, I saw her drinking tea, under the shelter of a garden awning.

As I approached she regarded me with a cold, haughty stare.

'I was under the impression, Mr Wallace, that I told you to telephone before you came here.'

'I did. You were out. So here I am.'

There was a chair near hers so I sat down.

'Well?' She put down her half-finished cup of tea and continued to stare at me.

'I have been instructed by my people to report progress to you and ask if you wish the investigation to go further.'

She stiffened.

'What progress?'

'You hired me to find out if your daughter is being blackmailed and, if so, by whom,' I said carefully. 'I saw your daughter collect the money from the bank. I followed her to a slum quarter on the waterfront. She left her car and entered the Black Cassette Disco. She remained there for ten minutes or so, then left without the money.'

Mrs Thorsen sat as if turned to stone.

'The Black Cassette? What is that?' Her voice was harsh.

'It is an all-black night-club. No whites are allowed.'

'Yet you say my daughter went in there?'

'Obviously she was paying someone in the club the ten thousand dollars. That doesn't mean she associates with blacks, Mrs Thorsen.'

'Then what does it mean?'

'For all I know she may be contributing to a black fund; helping certain blacks who are living rough. I don't know. But I do know that this club is owned by Hank Smedley, the son of your butler.'

Once again she turned to stone. I had to admire her. I could see how shocked she was, but her self-control couldn't be faulted.

She sat for three long minutes, staring down at her beautiful hands.

'Hank Smedley,' she finally muttered, not looking at me. 'Yes, of course. He used to help in the garden. I noticed my daughter and he were getting too friendly. He used to play with her. This was Angela's growing-up period. She liked to romp and be stupid, and Hank, who was ten years older than she, encouraged her. I complained to my husband. He got rid of Hank. For a time Angela seemed to miss him.' She drew in a deep breath. 'So it would seem that she still meets him, and now gives him money. How dreadful!'

'It looks like that, but it may not be so.'

'I must talk to my butler about this!' Her voice turned savage and she glared at me.

'It would be better, Mrs Thorsen, for you first to talk to your daughter.'

'To Angela?' She gave a bitter laugh. 'She wouldn't tell me anything. I really believe she hates me.'

'There are complications, Mrs Thorsen,' I said. 'I haven't been wasting your money,' I said. 'If you want me to go further with this, then it is up to you. Just tell me, and my agency will either close the case or continue it.'

'What complications?'

I certainly wasn't going to bring her son onto the scene at this stage.

'Hank is dangerous, Mrs Thorsen,' I said. 'I would like to find out what is going on in his club. The police have tried, but have got nowhere. If I can find enough evidence of wrong-doing, I want to put this man behind bars. This is now up to you.'

There was a cruel, hard look on her gaunt face as she said, 'Nothing would please me more than to know that useless scum is in prison! Very well! I don't care how much it costs! Continue the investigation!'

'I will do that, but only on one condition, Mrs Thorsen,' I said, getting to my feet. 'I ask you to say nothing about this to your daughter nor to your butler. Is that understood?'

'I leave it to you to put that animal behind bars!' she said, and the viciousness in her voice was startling. 'I leave it to you, and you take the responsibility!'

On that note, I left her.

4

I sat in my car outside the Thorsens' residence, listening to the steady rain drumming on the roof of my car. I turned over in my mind the conversation I had had with Mrs Thorsen. At least she had given the agency the green light to go ahead with the investigation. As it was costing her, I decided she must get value for money.

I drove slowly along the high wall that encircled the estate. As I expected, I came on a narrow lane to my right, and I drove up it, still seeing the high wall. I hoped this lane would lead directly to the cottage where Angela Thorsen lived, and I was right.

Leaving the car on the wet grass verge and struggling into my mac, I walked up the short tarmac drive until I saw the cottage: small, probably three bedrooms and a big living-room. Standing before the cottage was Angela's beat-up, rusty Beatle car.

I arrived at the front door. There was no porch. As I pressed the bell, the rain dripped down on me.

The door jerked open. I was confronted by a large black woman who looked big enough, tough enough and strong enough to give Larry Holmes a work-out.

She looked me up and down, then demanded in a harsh voice, 'What do you want, mister?'

'Miss Angela Thorsen,' I said, staring directly at her.

'On your way, mister. Miss Angela doesn't see strangers. Beat it!'

I had my professional card ready and I poked it at her.

'She'll see me,' I said in my cop voice. 'Let's have some action! I'm getting wet!'

She read the card, stared at me, then snapped, 'Wait!' and slammed the door.

So this was Hanna Smedley. I felt sorry for Josh. No wonder he had taken to the bottle. I stood there in the rain and waited.

Five minutes crawled by. By then, I was exasperated. I put my finger on the bell-push and leaned on it. That produced some action. The door jerked open, and Mrs Smedley glared at me.

'Well, come in! Take that mac off. I don't want the place sopping wet.'

I took off my mac and hat and dropped them in a puddle of rain on the floor of the lobby.

She opened a door and waved me in, so I entered a large living-room, comfortably furnished with lounging chairs and a big TV set.

I took this in with a quick glance, then turned my attention to the girl who was sitting in a lounging chair, looking enquiringly at me.

Angela Thorsen wasn't wearing her sun-goggles or her concealing hat. The dim light from the rain-filled sky fell directly on her.

I was startled. When I had asked her mother if Angela had boy-friends, I remembered her exact words: 'Most unlikely. I can't imagine any decent boy being interested in Angela. As I have said, she is not attractive.'

Mother's jealousy?

I looked at this girl. She reminded me of Audrey Hepburn when she first appeared on the screen: the same classical features, the dark hair, the serious, dark brown eyes. OK, she had a starvation body, but shift your eyes to her face, you found sexual attraction.

'Excuse me for intruding, Miss Thorsen,' I said. 'I am hoping you can help me.'

She smiled and waved me to a chair.

'I hope I can, Mr Wallace. Please sit down. Would you like tea or coffee?'

'No thanks.' I sat down.

'You are a private detective?' I saw she was holding my card.

'That's correct, Miss Thorsen.'

'It must be an exciting life. I often read thrillers about private detectives.'

'A private detective's life is far from thrilling except in books, Miss Thorsen,' I said. 'Most of my time is spent sitting in cars or talking to people who don't co-operate.'

Again she smiled.

'So you have come to me. Please, tell me why.'

'I have been hired to find your brother.' I was watching her, but her smile didn't slip. She just looked interested.

'My brother? Terry?'

'That's right. An old lady has left him money, and unless he is found, the money remains in the bank. I have been hired to find him.'

'An old lady has left Terry money?'

'Yes; Miss Thorsen.'

'How nice of her. Who is she?'

I put on my mournful look.

'That's why my job is so dull,' I said. 'My boss just tells me to find Terry Thorsen as he has been left money by an old lady. He doesn't tell me her name, but he did tell me she has left your brother one hundred thousand dollars. So I am making enquiries.'

She leaned forward.

'Did you say one hundred thousand dollars?'

'That's correct, Miss Thorsen.'

She sat back and gave me her guileless smile.

'How nice.'

'Wonderful for him,' I said, 'but I still have to find him. Can you help me?'

'I wish I could. I haven't seen my brother for months.'

'He hasn't written to you or telephoned you?'

'No.' Her smile was replaced by a sad expression. 'It

grieves me, Mr Wallace. At one time, my brother and I were close.'

I couldn't decide if she was telling me the truth, but if not, she was lying with impressive expertise.

'Perhaps you know of a friend of his who would give me a lead,' I suggested.

Sadly, she shook her head.

'I don't know any of his friends.'

'I guess you know he was playing the piano at the Dead End club, then suddenly left.'

Her eyes opened a trifle in what could have been surprise.

'No, I didn't know that.'

'So you can give me no help?'

'I wish I could. I have your card. If I do hear from Terry, I will telephone you.'

I got to my feet.

'I'd be glad if you would do that. It's a shame. There's this large amount of money in the bank, and your brother isn't aware it is his.'

She nodded, then got to her feet.

'It is a shame.'

Then I produced the question that would tell me if she was an expert liar or was speaking the truth.

Watching her closely, I said, 'Do you happen to know where I can locate Hank Smedley?'

If I hadn't been watching her so closely, I would have missed the slight flicker of her eyes, and the slight tightening of her guileless smile. I knew for sure I had got under her guard.

A slight pause, then her smile came into place as she said, 'Hank Smedley? How surprising. You mean the black boy who once worked in our garden?'

'That's right, Miss Thorsen. Hank, who is Mrs Smedley's son. Do you know where I can locate him?'

'I don't.' Again the guileless smile. 'I haven't seen him for a long time, nor has his mother.'

Then I knew she was lying, and had been lying with an

expertise I had not encountered before. She could easily have fooled me but for the fact I had seen her walk into the Black Cassette.

I too could put on an act. I lifted my shoulders in a resigned shrug.

'Looks like your brother is going to be hard to find.' I gave her my hard cop stare, 'But we keep on digging, Miss Thorsen. When my agency is hired for a job, we don't give up until the job is nicely finished. I am sure you will be interested to know when we do find your brother.' I smiled at her. 'I will let you know.'

Leaving her standing motionless, her smile now gone, I went out into the lobby, picked up my mac, slapped on my wet hat and walked down the tarmac to my car.

Retarded, her mother had told me. Unattractive?

This girl, around 24 years of age, was the finest liar I had ever questioned. What a mug she had nearly made of me! If I hadn't asked her about Hank, I would have had every reason to believe the lies she had been telling me.

I slid into my car.

As I started the motor, I wondered what she was going to do? Alert her brother? Alert Hank? Perhaps do nothing.

I reversed the car and drove down to the highway.

Back in my office, I found Bill thumping on his typewriter.

I told him of my interview with Angela, then concluded, 'Here we have a real character. She lies beautifully, she has steel nerves, she has sex, she pretends she doesn't know where to locate her brother, and bluntly says she hasn't seen Hank Smedley for years.'

'I still don't understand why you want to find the brother,' Bill said. 'Hank seems to me to be the leading character in this business.'

'Maybe you're right,' I said, pulling my typewriter towards me, 'but I have a hunch that Terry could be the key. I could be wrong. Let's get these reports off the desk.'

It was around 19.20 by the time we had completed our reports, and I had put them away in the Thorsen file.

'What now?' Bill asked.

'We'll go eat Italian,' I said, 'then I am going to talk to Hank Smedley.'

Bill cocked his head on one side.

'You're going to that all-black club?'

'That's what I'm going to do.'

'Fine, and I'm coming with you.'

I unlocked the bottom drawer of my desk and took out my .38 gun. I checked it and then thrust it into my trouser belt.

'Get your gun too, Bill,' I said. 'We could walk into trouble.'

He unlocked his drawer and produced a pair of brass knuckle-dusters. He slid them on each hand and surveyed them with loving eyes.

'If you have a gun, Dirk, I don't need a gun.'

'Hey! Those things are illegal!'

'That's a fact. So they are illegal.' He took them off and dripped them into his pocket. 'Nothing like a lump of brass if one gets into a fight with a black.'

I shrugged. I knew he had a punch that would put a mule to sleep. With those lethal bits of brass, he could put an elephant to sleep.

'I have a phone call to make, then we take off.' I called the Bellevue Hotel. I was lucky to catch Suzy. She sounded breathless. I could hear the sound of voices as people converged on the reception desk.

'Just a word, love,' I said. 'Thanks for putting the wall right and for the locks. You are marvellous!'

'That makes two of us, my hero. Keep out of trouble. See you next Wednesday,' and she hung up.

Leaving the office, Bill and I went down to the car. It was still drizzling. I drove to Secombe's main street, fought for parking, then we walked to Lucino's restaurant.

I often dined there, and Lucino, squat, enormously fat

and more Italian than the Italians, beamed a welcome. We shook hands, said this and that, then he conducted us to a corner table. At this early hour, the restaurant was nearly empty.

'The special, Lucino,' I said as I sat down.

'For you, Mr Wallace, the *very* special.'

He brought us a rough Italian wine, poured the drinks, then went away.

'If we come out of this disco alive,' Bill said, 'what's the next move?'

'We go in there as Acme operators,' I said. 'I ask to see Hank. If by then there isn't a rough house, and if Hank shows up, I am asking him if he can help us to find Terry. Do you now see how important Terry is to this investigation?'

Bill scratched his head.

'I guess so,' he said doubtfully. 'I see he gets you around.'

'That's the idea. So you ask what's the next move to be. This depends on how co-operative Hank is. I doubt if he'll tell us anything. So the next move is we latch on to Angela, and follow her from the moment she gets up to the moment she goes to bed.'

Bill nodded. This was the kind of work he liked.

'Think you'll get something from that?'

'I don't know, but it's worth a try.'

Lucino came to the table bearing a vast platter of spaghetti, decorated with crisp, fried octopus, pieces of chicken and shrimps. Hot plates were produced and a big bowl of sauce that smelt of garlic and tomatoes was planked down on the table.

'The best, Mr Wallace,' Lucino said, beaming. 'Nothing but the best for you.'

We ate. Both of us were hungry. When there was nothing left, we sat back and looked at each other.

'Ready for a possible rough house, Bill?' I asked.

He grinned.

'After that meal, I'm ready to take on the Marines.'

The time was 20.15 A little early for the Black Cassette to be in action.

I drove down to the waterfront, found a parking space, then we walked the rest of the way to the disco. As we reached the shoddy entrance to the club, I eased my gun for a quick draw. I saw Bill had his hands in his pockets.

I shoved open the door and we walked into a large room, furnished with small tables against the walls, a polished dance floor in the centre and, at the end of the room, a bar.

There was a distinct smell of reefer smoke hanging in the air. As I had thought, the action hadn't started, but there were a number of black people: men and women, sitting at some of the tables drinking beer.

Three men, one holding a trumpet, one holding a sax and the third one setting up a drum set, were on a raised platform.

The whole outfit looked respectable enough.

There was a sudden, solid silence as we walked in. In a moment a big black came sliding out of the shadows and blocked our further entrance. He looked big enough and powerful enough to knock over a bull.

'Can't you guys read?' he demanded in a harsh, loud voice.

'Move over, black boy,' I said. 'I want to talk to Hank.'

His bloodshot eyes flickered.

'No white trash in here!'

'Can *you* read?' I said, and shoved my professional card at him.

The card made an impression on him. He stared at it, and I saw his thick lips move as he read.

'You a cop?' he asked, his voice less harsh.

'Look, black boy,' I barked, 'take that card to Hank and tell him I want to talk to him. Get moving!'

He hesitated, then shambled away, walking across the dance floor to a door he opened, then disappeared from sight.

The dozen or so blacks were watching all this. None of them moved nor spoke. I guess they thought we were cops.

I wasn't going to let my advantage rest.

'Come on,' I said to Bill and walked across the dance floor,

58

pushed open the door through which the black had disappeared and found myself in a dimly lit corridor which led to another door. As I walked down the corridor, followed by Bill, the far end door jerked open.

I was confronted by Hank Smedley.

Bill had described him, but I didn't realize until I was facing him just how big he was. He wasn't big: he was enormous, standing some six feet seven inches high, with shoulders as wide as a barn door. Bill had said he had a small head: this was correct. Hank had a tiny head, ugly, flat broad nose, leathery-looking lips and glittering blood-shot eyes. He was the perfect model for a horror movie.

'What do you want?' he rasped, blocking the doorway. He had fists like hams, and they were clenched at his sides.

In a mild voice I said, 'Mr Hank Smedley?'

This seemed to throw him. Probably no white man had called him 'mister' before. His fists unclenched.

'Yeah. What you want?'

'I am from the Acme Detective Agency, Mr Smedley,' I said, still keeping the mild tone. 'I'm hoping you can help me.'

He stared suspiciously at me. I could almost hear what brain he had creaking.

'Help?' he finally snarled. 'I don't help white men. On your way. You stink up my place.'

'Let's cut out the black man, white man shit,' I said. 'My name is Wallace. So I call you Hank, and you call me Wallace. That way we might be able to have a civilized talk.'

This approach wasn't his scene. I could see him, hesitating. He was trying to make up his moronic mind whether to hit me or just stand there.

He stood there.

'I'm looking for Terry Zeigler,' I said, slowly and distinctly as if speaking to a child.

That got a reaction. He leaned forward, glaring at me. Right at that moment he made King Kong look like a powder-puff.

'What do you want with him?' he demanded.

I looked beyond him to where the black I had first spoken to was lurking and listening.

'Tell that boy to get the hell out,' I said. 'This is confidential.'

I was deliberately trying to impose my will on this ape.

It worked.

He turned around.

'Beat it!' he snarled.

The black shoved by me and went back into the main room.

'I'm trying to find Terry,' I said, 'because someone has left him a heap of jack. Unless I find him, the loot will remain in the bank.'

A spark of intelligence lit up his bloodshot eyes.

'How much?'

'Could be a hundred thousand. I don't know for sure.'

'A hundred thousand!' he exclaimed, staring at me. I could see money would always make an impact on him.

'That's what I understand. I won't swear to the amount: it could be more. Where do I find him?'

Blue-black veins stood out on his forehead as he thought.

Finally, he said, 'So what happens if you do find him?'

'No problem. I take him to the bank, he signs a few forms, and the money is his. It's as simple as that.'

He scratched his head while he continued to batter his brain.

'A hundred thousand?' he said. 'That's a lot of jack.'

'It sure is. Where do I find him?'

'I dunno where he is, but I might find out. I could ask around. For all I know he isn't living here. He could be anywhere.'

I had a feeling he was lying, but this had to be a patient game.

'OK, Hank,' I said. 'You have my card. If you do contact Terry, and he wants the money, give me a call. OK?'

60

'Yeah.'

He looked beyond me and became aware of Bill who was lolling against the wall, chewing gum.

'Who's that midget?' he demanded.

'He's my bodyguard,' I said, dead-pan. 'He's a good man to have around if smart boys think they're tough.'

'That little jerk?' Hank gave a wide, sneering grin. 'Man! He couldn't blow froth off beer.'

Seeing Bill slide his hands into his pockets, I backed away. I wanted to get out of this dump in one piece.

'Let's go, Bill,' I said sharply. 'OK, Hank, if you locate Terry let me know,' and taking a firm grip on Bill's arm, I walked him across the dance floor and into the bustle and humid heat of the waterfront.

'Why didn't you let me hang one on that ape?' Bill demanded as we reached my car.

'Patience,' I said, getting into the car. 'You'll have your chance, but not right now.'

As I drove away from the waterfront Bill asked. 'What's the next move?'

'We go home,' I said. 'I still think Terry could give us the key to this case. I've hung out two baits. Angela and Hank now know that Terry is worth a hundred thousand. I'm sure they know where he is. I'm hoping one of them will tell him and he'll surface.'

'Suppose they don't know where he is?'

'I think they do. We'll see. We'll meet at the office tomorrow at nine.'

Bill shrugged.

'Suits me.'

I dropped him off at his walk-up, then drove to the Bellevue Hotel.

Suzy gave me a loving smile as I crossed the lobby to the reception desk.

'Honey, how about tonight? Any time?' I asked.

She shook her head.

'Impossible tonight, Dirk, dear. I won't be free until

three. By then I'll be half dead. Be patient, my love. Wednesday as usual.'

Two fat elderly men came to the desk, and with a bright smile Suzy joined them.

I tramped back to my car and drove home. With junk on the TV, I took a shower and went to bed.

In the office, the following morning, around 09.30 with Bill at his desk and me at mine, the telephone bell rang.

I scooped up the receiver.

'Wallace?' I recognized Hank's gravelly voice.

'Hi, Hank,' I said and motioned to Bill who snatched up the extension so he could listen in. 'You got news for me?'

'Yeah.' A pause, then he went on, 'I found him, and he wants the money fast.'

'Where did you find him, Hank?'

A long pause, then he said, 'Never mind. When does he get the money?'

'No problem, Hank,' I said and grinned at Bill. 'I'll get it organized. I'll call you back.'

'What do you mean – organized?'

'I'll have to contact the bank and fix an appointment. Mr Ackland, who runs the bank, will need identification and time to prepare forms for Terry to sign. No problem. I'll call you back,' and I hung up.

'Stinks of a con,' Bill said as he hung up.

'Maybe. OK, here's what you do. Go, see that Harry Rich of the Dead End club and ask him if he will be willing to identify Terry at the bank. I think he will be there pronto, to see Terry again. You take care of that. I'll take care of Ackland.'

Twenty minutes later, I walked into Ackland's office. He rose from his desk, shook hands and gave me his benign bishop's smile.

'How do we progress, Mr Wallace?' he asked as we both sat down.

'I understand that you hold a hundred thousand dollars in

the favour of Terrance Thorsen or Zeigler, left him by a Miss Angus of the Breakers building.'

He stared at me.

'That is correct, but I don't understand, Mr Wallace. I am in touch with a Mr Lewis who is Miss Angus's executor, and until he finds Mr Thorsen, who appears to have disappeared, the money remains in the bank. What is this to do with your investigation?'

'I am hoping that Terrance Thorsen could be helpful, Mr Ackland. He has been told by friends that he can pick up this large sum of money, and it seems he has appeared. Up to now, he has not been in evidence, but the amount of money due to him brings him to the surface.'

'Extraordinary,' Ackland muttered.

'Have you ever met Terry Thorsen?'

Ackland looked startled.

'No. I've never seen him.'

'So when a man walks into your office claiming a hundred thousand dollars you wouldn't know if he was Terry Thorsen?'

Ackland half rose out of his chair, then sat back.

'You mean there could be an imposter?'

'Well, a hundred thousand – it isn't peanuts.'

'Of course, I would need identification.'

'It occurred to me, Mr Ackland, the best identification you could have is to invite Miss Angela Thorsen to attend, and if she identifies her brother, there should be no problem.'

His fat face brightened.

'That is a very constructive idea, Mr Wallace.'

'Could we set this up sometime this afternoon?'

'Well – ' He looked at his appointment book. 'Yes, perhaps, around three o'clock.'

'Would you telephone Miss Thorsen to see if she will come? I expect she will be happy to see her brother again.'

'Yes, of course. I want to do everything I can to help the Thorsen family. Let me see if I can reach her.' He pressed a button and told Miss Kertch to connect him with Miss Angela Thorsen.

There was a good five-minute wait while I smoked a cigarette and Ackland turned papers around on his desk. When the call came through, he was all oil.

'This is Horace Ackland of the Pacific & National Bank. I do hope I am not disturbing you.'

He listened, nodded, then went on, 'I don't know if you are aware that your brother, Terrance, has inherited a hundred thousand dollars.'

He listened again, then went on, 'Yes. Mr Wallace has been most helpful. Now, Miss Thorsen, it is necessary to make sure the man who is claiming all this money is your brother. This is, of course, red tape, but as I have never met nor seen your brother I need him to be identified. Would you be prepared to come here at three o'clock this afternoon and identify your brother for me?'

He listened nodding.

'Yes, I can understand that. It is a long time since you have seen him. I understand that you will be pleased to see him again. Splendid! Then I will expect you at my office at three o'clock this afternoon. Thank you, Miss Thorsen,' and he hung up.

Looking at me, he said, 'Of course, she will be only too happy to co-operate. I see no problem.'

I felt sorry for him. Horace Ackland didn't know Angela Thorsen as I did.

'Fine,' I said, and got to my feet. 'I'll be here at three o'clock.'

'Do that, Mr Wallace.' He rose to his feet and, leaning across his desk, shook hands. 'This should be a very interesting meeting.'

'I guess so. See you later,' and I left him.

At 14.45, I walked into the Pacific & National Bank and gave Miss Kertch my friendly smile, which bounced off her like a golf ball flung against a concrete wall.

'Mr Ackland is engaged,' she snapped.

'OK. Just tell him I'm here.' I walked to a lounging chair and made myself comfortable.

I have always found banks offer a lot of interest. I watched people come and go. I watched fat old women putting money into their bags. I watched them chat up the teller, who had a fixed, kindly smile for each of the old trouts as they arrived. Banking was not for me, I decided.

Bill and I had had a scratch lunch. He had told me he had seen not only Harry Rich but also a Miss Liza Manchini, his receptionist, who had been Terry's girl-friend at the time of his disappearance.

'Great stuff, Bill. A really nice bit of probing, and dead on time.'

'No problem,' he said, chewing on his hamburger. 'Rich wants to talk to Terry. He's hoping he can persuade him to return to his club. Liza is panting to get Terry back into bed. Both of them will play.'

'Fine. Collect them, Bill, and bring them to the bank at 15.20. Not before. I want them to be a surprise.'

After a ten-minute wait Miss Kertch said, 'Mr Ackland is free now.'

I got up and entered Ackland's office. As usual, he shook hands and beamed his bishop's smile.

'Well, Mr Wallace, this should be most interesting,' he said, waving me to a chair. 'It's not often I have an affair like this.' He shifted in his chair. 'I have all the necessary papers. I have spoken to Mr Lewis. When Miss Thorsen identifies her brother the matter can be finalized.'

I lit a cigarette, then relaxed back in the chair.

At exactly 15.00, the buzzer on Ackland's desk sounded.

I heard Miss Kertch's voice squawk, 'Mr Terry Thorsen is here.'

'Send him in,' Ackland said, then beamed at me. 'This will be more than interesting.'

'You can say that yet again,' I said.

The door opened, and a man around 25 or so walked in.

He was wearing a white shirt, and black trousers tucked into Mexican boots. His black hair was long to his shoulders. He was thin and had a lean, rat-like face with small, black suspicious eyes.

Beaming, Ackland got to his feet.

'Mr Thorsen?'

'Yeah,' the man said, then stared at me. 'Who's this?'

'I am representing your interests,' I said, getting to my feet. 'The name's Wallace. I am working with Mr Solly Lewis who is the late Miss Angus's attorney.'

His eyes shifted and he stared at Ackland.

'Well, come on. I'm in a hurry. Where's the money?' His voice was harsh and his bearing hostile.

Ackland flinched.

'Naturally, Mr Thorsen, I will require identification before giving you the money.' He had lost his bishop's smile.

'What do you mean?' There was a snarl in the voice, then the buzzer sounded.

'Miss Thorsen, Mr Ackland,' Miss Kertch squawked.

'Your sister, Mr Thorsen,' Ackland said. 'I am sure you will be glad to see her again.'

The door opened and Angela Thorsen entered. She was wearing the sweat-shirt, blue jeans, the Mexican hat and the big sun-goggles. She paused in the doorway, then moved directly to the man claiming to be Terry Thorsen.

'Terry!' she exclaimed. 'This is marvellous! How long it has been!'

'Yeah,' the man who was claiming to be Thorsen said. 'Look, we'll talk later. I want the money, and then let's get the hell out of here.'

She nodded.

'Of course, Terry.' She turned to Ackland who was now standing and beaming. 'This is my brother. Will you pay him, please? I want to have a long talk with him.'

'Certainly, Miss Thorsen. You do identify him?' Ackland said.

'I said so, didn't I?' There was a hard snap in her voice. 'I want to talk to my brother!'

Looking flustered, Ackland pushed some papers across his desk.

'If you would sign these, Mr Thorsen, then I will arrange immediate payment.' Ackland was falling over himself to give Angela Thorsen service. 'How would you like the money?'

'In cash,' the long-haired man snarled, snatching the pen Ackland offered, and scrawled on the lines Ackland pointed out.

While he was doing this I went to the door and looked out. I saw Bill waiting with two people who were clearly Harry Rich and Liza Manchini.

'Mr Rich, please,' I said, and signalled to Bill to hold back Miss Manchini. It looked like he'd have his work cut out.

Harry Rich, immaculately dressed, moved into Ackland's office.

Ackland looked bewildered.

'Who is this gentleman?' he asked.

'This is Mr Harry Rich who owns a night-club, Mr Ackland,' I said. 'He employed Mr Thorsen as a pianist. Mr Thorsen was then known as Terry Zeigler. I thought it would be constructive for Mr Rich to identify Mr Thorsen before you parted with the money.'

'But Miss Thorsen has already identified him!' Ackland spluttered.

I turned to Rich.

'Is this man Terry Zeigler?'

Rich stared hard at the long-haired man, then he shook his head.

'He dresses the way Terry dressed, but he is not Terry. I don't know who the hell he is, but he is not Terry Zeigler.'

'Sure of that, Mr Rich?'

'Of course, I am sure. Terry worked for me for months. I paid his wages into his hand every week. I don't know what you're trying but you have been wasting my time, Wallace,' and Rich walked out.

Without giving Ackland time to recover from this shock, I went to the door and signalled to Bill.

'This is Miss Manchini,' I said. 'She lived with Terry Thorsen, known to her as Terry Zeigler, for quite a time.' I turned to Liza who had swept forward, her face alight with anticipation of seeing Terry again. Then she stopped short, staring at the man with the long hair who was glaring at her. 'Miss Manchini,' I said, 'is this man Terry Zeigler?'

Her frustration and disappointment were too genuine to doubt.

'That slob! Terry! Do you imagine I wouldn't know Terry when I see him again?'

'You are saying this man is not Terry Zeigler?' I said.

'Yes! Do you think I would go to bed with a slob like this?' Her voice became shrill. 'God! I thought I was going to see Terry again,' and she began to cry.

Bill, who was standing by her, took a firm grip on her arm and led her out.

There was a long pause. I looked at the man who was claiming to be Terry. Sweat was running down his face, and his eyes burned with fury. I looked at Angela Thorsen. She was motionless, hidden behind her sun-goggles. I looked at Ackland who sat in a heap as if his spine was broken.

As I expected, Angela was the first to recover and take the initiative. She walked up to Ackland's desk and stood over him.

'Mr Ackland,' she said, her voice harsh, 'I know this man is my brother. Are you going to tell me you are going to take the word of a cheap night-club owner and a whore against mine?'

Nice work, I thought, seeing Ackland's reaction.

'Of course not, Miss Thorsen, but there must be some mistake,' he mumbled.

'There is no mistake!' Angela snapped. 'These two people don't want Terry to have the money left to him! They are deliberately lying! Please arrange for my brother to be paid!'

I came to Ackland's rescue. He looked as if he was going to have a stroke.

'Miss Thorsen!' I barked in my cop voice. 'Mr Ackland has no authority to pay out this money! I am representing Mr Lewis who is the executor of Miss Angus's will. I am not satisfied. You say this man is your brother. Two people, who have known your brother for some time, say this man is an imposter. Mr Ackland will not be given the authority to pay out one hundred thousand dollars until I am satisfied this man is really your brother.'

She turned. I longed to hook off her big sun-goggles that completely masked her face, but I could see by her thin, trembling body how furious she was.

'I demand my brother gets the money!' she said, her voice low and full of hate.

'There is really no problem,' I said. 'Across the road is the Eden Club. Suppose we all go over there, and I will arrange with the owner, who is a friend of mine, for this guy to sit at the piano and play. If he plays as well as Fats Waller, then he gets the money. Fair enough?'

The man trying to pass himself off as Terry Zeigler suddenly went berserk.

'I told that fucking slob it wouldn't work!' he yelled. 'I told you, you stupid bitch, it wouldn't work!' and shoving by me, he rushed out of the office.

'Well, Mr Ackland, that seems to be that,' I said, feeling sorry for him as he sat deflated, his fat face as white as a sheet. 'When Terry Thorsen does turn up, I'll alert you.' I looked at Angela who was standing like a statue. 'A good try, Miss Thorsen, but not good enough.'

She turned slowly.

'I will make you sorry for this,' she said, her voice a low hiss. 'God! You will be sorry!'

The vicious menace in her voice was unmistakable.

'Try to grow up, Miss Thorsen,' I said quietly. 'Money isn't everything,' and I left the office, feeling sorry for Ackland who now had this vicious girl to cope with.

I expected to find Bill waiting for me, but he wasn't there. I walked to where I had parked my car. That wasn't there either. I flagged down a cab and returned to the office.

I had quite a report to write up for the Thorsen file.

5

I was expecting to find Bill at his desk, but he wasn't there, so I put a phone call through to Solly Lewis, Miss Angus's executor.

He answered on the first ring and sounded like a man hopefully needing a rich client.

'Solly Lewis, attorney,' he announced in a firm, determined voice.

'Who else?' I said. 'This is Wallace. Acme.'

'Oh.' A disappointed pause, then 'Yes, Mr Wallace?' His voice had gone down two major tones.

'You busy?'

'Not right now. What is it?'

'Relax, Mr Lewis, and listen.' I then gave him a blow-by-blow account of the afternoon's performance at the bank. He listened in complete silence, then I concluded, 'Looks, Mr Lewis, that Miss Angus's money is attracting flies.'

'I don't understand,' he said 'Miss Thorsen identified this man as her brother.'

'Don't let us waste time. I've given you the facts. Have you ever seen Terry Thorsen?'

'No, I haven't.'

'I told Ackland you would not release the money unless you had complete assurance that the claimant was Terry Thorsen. Right?'

'The money was left to Terry Zeigler, Mr Wallace.'

'From my information,' I said patiently 'Thorsen and Zeigler are one and the same.'

'I don't know. All I do know is the money has been left to a man called Terry Zeigler.' A pause, then he went on, 'What information have you that Thorsen and Zeigler are the same?'

71

Patiently, I explained that When Terry left home he got a job playing the piano at the Dead End Club, and changed his name to Zeigler.

'Very well, Mr Wallace,' Lewis said. 'Then I can assume that Thorsen and Zeigler are one and the same.'

'That's what you can do. Now tell me: if Zeigler is dead or is never found, who gets the money?'

'Miss Angus left the money to him. No one will get it unless it can be proved without doubt that Zeigler was Thorsen, then Thorsen's next of kin gets it.'

'Would that be his mother or his sister?'

'His mother.'

'OK, Mr Lewis. We'll keep in contact. Maybe it would be an idea for you to call Ackland and tell him the money stays in the bank until you are satisfied about the claimant. OK?'

'I'll do that right now.'

'Fine. I'll be talking to you again, Mr Lewis,' and I hung up.

The time now was 16.15. I wondered where Bill had got to. I wanted to discuss with him this new development. I pulled my typewriter towards me and began to thump out my report.

I had just finished when Bill walked in.

Whipping the last page from my typewriter, I said, 'Where've you been? I thought you had dropped dead.'

'I could do with a drink,' he said as he slumped into his desk chair. 'Where've I been? I've been working my ass off.'

I produced the office bottle, noting the time now was 18.40. I made two drinks, found ice and shoved a glass over to Bill.

'So?'

'When this guy, pretending to be Terry, came charging out of Ackland's office, I could see he was crazy mad. I followed him into the street. He had one of these big souped-up Honda motor cycles, and he took off. He was

72

heading for the waterfront, and it was my guess he was going to the Black Cassette, but I was wrong. He drove past the joint, went further, then turned up Oyster Alley. There are three blocks of walk-ups there, used by the waterfront fishermen. I didn't drive in. I heard the Honda engine die. By the time I had parked the car and walked up the alley there was no sign of this guy, but his Honda was parked outside a sleazy-looking building. I took the number of the Honda, then drove to the car registration office. No problem there. The guy's name is Lu Gerando, living at apartment 10,3 Oyster Alley.'

Bill paused to take a long drink at his Scotch. 'So I went along to the cop house and had a talk to Joe Beigler. He wanted to know what my interest was in Gerando. I said I was just asking for information and did he know anything about the guy. He said he knew of him, but he was clean so far as the cops were concerned. All the same, the cops were keeping an eye on him. His father worked for the Mafia. He must have crossed his lines because he was blown away when Lu was 15 years old. He took care of his mother by doing casual labour on the waterfront until she died. They are Sicilians, and Beigler is suspicious of Gerando, but has nothing to pin onto him. I went back to the waterfront and contacted a couple of guys I know down there, but they could tell me nothing. They don't know what Gerando does for a living.' Bill finished his drink. 'That's it, Dirk.'

'Good progress, Bill,' I said. 'I'll talk to Al Barney. He could come up with something.'

The intercom buzzed. I pressed the switch.

'Dirk?' Glenda snapped. 'Bring the Thorsen file, please,' and she switched off.

Bill and I exchanged glances, then I got the file.

'So what's eating her?' I said as I made for the door.

I entered Glenda's office and put the file on her desk.

'Right up to date,' I said.

'Colonel Parnell will be back tomorrow morning,' Glenda said. 'He will want to see this,' she tapped the file. 'The investigation is finished. I had a telephone call from Mrs Thorsen. She said she was not paying us any more fees, and she was no longer interested. So, Dirk you can forget the Thorsen case.'

I stared at her.

'You mean all this is so much waste of time?' I slammed my fist down on the file.

Glenda smiled.

'We've done very nicely out of Mrs Thorsen. I wouldn't call it a waste of time.'

'Just when it began to look interesting.' I shrugged. 'So, OK. What's the next assignment?'

'That's for the colonel to decide. You'll be seeing him tomorrow.'

I returned to my office and broke the news to Bill.

'Oh, for God's sake!' he exclaimed in disgust.

'That makes two of us,' I said. 'Well, there it is. The colonel will find us something else to work on.' I looked at my watch. The time was 19.20. 'Let's go and eat. How about Lucino again?'

Bill's face brightened.

'Great! Let's go!'

Then the telephone bell on my desk came alive. Impatiently, I snatched up the receiver. I was hungry and depressed, but I wasn't to know this telephone call would alter my whole way of life.

'Dirk Wallace,' I snapped. 'Who is this?'

'Oh, Dirk!' A woman's quavering voice. 'This is Betty Stowell.'

Betty Stowell was the third receptionist at the Bellevue Hotel. She and Suzy were close friends. I had met Betty from time to time: a nice, cuddly girl with no complexes, a steady boy-friend and hopes of raising a big family.

'Hi, Betty,' I said, then stiffened as I could hear she was crying. 'For God's sake, Betty, what's the trouble?'

'Oh, Dirk. God forgive me for having to tell you, but someone must tell you. Oh, Dirk . . .'

74

Cold sweat began to run down my back.

'Is it Suzy?'

'Yes, dear Dirk. Suzy is dead.'

'What are you telling me?' I shouted. 'Suzy dead?'

'Yes.'

I sat motionless, listening to the sounds of her sobbing and knowing from these sounds there could be no mistake. *Suzy was dead!* Suzy whom I loved, planned to marry, who did so much for me – dead!

'What happened?' I shouted.

'Please – the police know. I can't talk any more,' and still sobbing, she hung up.

I closed my eyes.

Suzy dead!

Vaguely, I heard Bill say, 'Jesus! I'm sorry, Dirk,' and then he got up and left me alone. I was grateful for that. I sat, staring into space, thinking of Suzy, what she had meant to me, and realizing, perhaps for the first time, how much I loved her.

I sat there for maybe ten minutes, then I got hold of myself.

How did it happen?

I pulled the telephone to me and dialled police headquarters. I asked to speak to Joe Beigler. He and I had a good association. If anyone knew, he would.

He came on the line.

'Joe, this is Dirk Wallace,' I said.

'Look, Dirk, I'm just signing off. Can't it wait until tomorrow?'

'Suzy Long,' I said. 'What happened?'

'What's she to you?' Beigler demanded.

'She was my girl-friend, Joe. We were planning to get married. That's what she meant to me.'

'Oh! Christ, I'm sorry to hear that!'

'What happened?'

'The facts are these,' Beigler said. 'This morning as Miss Long was leaving for the hotel, a car pulled up and a man asked her if she could direct him to Westbury Drive. There were two old women passing and they heard this. Miss Long went up to the car and began to give directions. She got a face full of acid, and the car took off. These two old women say that Miss Long, covering her face and screaming, ran into the road and was crushed to death by a passing truck.'

I felt bile rise in my mouth and had a struggle not to vomit.

Beigler, understanding my feelings, gave me a long moment, then he said, 'The boys are working on this, but so far, they've turned up nothing. The two witnesses were old and useless. Neither of them could give a description of the car. One of them thought the drive was black, but her friend said she imagined that. The boys are questioning everyone living in the various blocks. They could come up with something.'

The driver was black.

I took a long, deep breath.

'Where is she?'

'The city's morgue.' A pause, then he went on, 'Look, Dirk, leave it. Miss Stowell has been most helpful. The staff manager of the hotel has identified Miss Log. We have informed her father who is flying here to take care of the funeral. Take my tip, Dirk, don't go look at her. The acid did a job, and so did the truck. Keep out of it.'

'Thanks, Joe,' I said and hung up.

He was right. I wanted to keep in my memory Suzy's bright, lovely face, not a face disfigured by acid. I told myself I wouldn't even go to the funeral. The dead are dead.

I sat back and lit a cigarette. This awful empty feeling of loss gradually turned into a burning feeling for revenge. I sat there for maybe twenty minutes before making my decision. Having made it, I locked my desk drawers, turned off the lights and walked down the corridor to the elevators.

I drove back to my apartment. As I paused outside my

front door, fumbling for my keys, I saw a scrap of paper pasted on the door.

On it, scrawled in small lettering was the message:

YOU WERE WARNED, SUCKER.

A full moon was climbing lazily into a cloudless sky as I found parking on the waterfront.

I had showered and changed into a sports shirt and linen slacks. I had checked my last bank statement. I was worth $12,000. This was money I had been saving for when Suzy and I set up home. No more Suzy – no more home.

I left the car and walked along the waterfront which was crowded with tourists, gaping at the various characters coming off the fishing boats.

The time was 21.30. The air was hot and humid, but, at least, there was no sign of rain.

I walked to the Neptune Tavern. There were a few fishermen at the tables, eating. This wasn't a tourist haunt. Across the room Al Barney, in his special corner, was eating, a beer at his elbow.

He put down his knife and fork as I sat down at his table. His fat face wore a mournful look.

'I was hoping to see you, Mr Wallace,' he said. 'Have something on the house.'

Sam, the barkeep, slid up.

'Accept a corned beef sandwich, Mr Wallace,' he said. 'You'll like it. My pleasure, please, and Mr Wallace, accept my sorrow.'

I looked at Barney.

'Yeah. The news is out. The acid job,' Barney said, and shook his head. 'Let me tell you, everyone who means anything down here is sorry. I am more than sorry.' He cut a slice of meat and shoved it into his mouth. Munching, he went on, 'Anything I can do?'

Sam slid up to the table and placed a fat sandwich and a glass half filled with Scotch and ice before me.

'My pleasure, Mr Wallace,' he said and slid away.

I waited while Barney continued to feed his face. After a couple of more mouthfuls, he put down his knife and fork.

'Mr Wallace, you have done me a lot of good in the past. I don't forget people who do things for me. Give me and Sam the pleasure to eat that sandwich. A guy works and thinks better when he has grub in his gut.'

So I ate the sandwich, which could have been worse, and I drank the Scotch. I was feeling a lot more like myself as I lit a cigarette.

Barney beamed at me.

'OK, Mr Wallace, I am at your service.'

'Al, I'm going to fix those bastards who did the acid job, but first, I need information.'

Barney nodded.

'When I heard about it, I reckoned you'd start something. So OK, what information?'

'Know anything about Lu Gerando?'

Barney stiffened, and his little eyes popped wide open.

'Gerando? Don't tell me he's mixed up in this, Mr Wallace.'

'He could be. What do you know about him?'

'No good,' Barney said. 'He stooges for Joe Walinski who owns a big yacht, and Gerando guards the yacht when Walinski is out of town. He drives Walinski's car. A general stooge.'

'Do you know if he is in any way connected with Hank Smedley?'

'I guess so. I've seen them together.' Barney sipped his beer. 'They certainly know each other.'

'Who is Joe Walinski?'

Barney shifted uneasily on his chair.

'Mr Wallace, you are getting me into deep water. I don't like talking about Walinski. It ain't healthy.' He was now looking worried.

I waited.

78

Barney made a signal to Sam who came rushing over with a plate of the ghastly sausages. He looked at me.

'Can I get you something else, Mr Wallace?' he asked. 'A nice cup of coffee or maybe another Scotch? It's all on the house.'

'Thanks, Sam. Nothing,' I said, trying to keep the edge of impatience out of my voice.

He took away the used plates and went back to the bar.

Barney fed three of the sausages into his mouth, gulped, wiped his watering eyes with the back of his hand, then regarded me.

'Mr Wallace, if I talk about Walinski and it gets known, I'm going to be found in the harbour with my throat cut.'

'If you don't tell anyone and I don't tell anyone, who's to know? Who is Joe Walinski?'

He ate three more sausages, coughed, again wiped his eyes, then leaning forward, breathing hot pepper in my face, he said, 'OK, Mr Wallace, so I talk. I wouldn't do it for any other man, but for you . . .'

'Who is Joe Walinski?' I repeated, a snarl in my voice.

'He is the collector for the east-coast Mafia. He comes in his yacht every first of the month and stays a week. During that week he collects protection money, blackmail money, the casino's pay-off. That's who Walinski is: as dangerous and as deadly as a dose of poison. Make no mistake about that, Mr Wallace. All the waterfront know what's going on, but they say nothing. The waterfront cops know, but they say nothing. On the night of the first of each month, around three in the morning, people arrive at the yacht with their pay-offs. The waterfront cops look the other way. No one goes near the yacht unless he or she is doing business with Walinski. No one!'

'What's the yacht called, Al?'

'The *Hermes*. Just beyond the fish trawlers to the right.'

'Is Hank Smedley one of Walinski's collectors?'

Barney tossed three more sausages into his mouth, munched, then nodded.

I have never seen him look so worried. I decided it wasn't fair to press him further so I got to my feet and offered him my hand. His grip was clammy, but sympathetic.

'I'm sorry, Mr Wallace. Please don't do anything crazy.'

I nodded and went over to Sam.

'Can't I pay?'

'Mr Wallace, I am sorry, like Mr Barney is. No, nothing to pay and good luck.'

I walked out into the dark, humid night and along the quay. The tourists had returned to their hotels for dinner. Only a few late fishermen were scattered around, talking. The two waterfront cops were standing, staring aimlessly at the trawlers. I regarded them closely. These two men were aware of Walinski's racket, and I was sure they had a pay-off to keep their mouths shut. They were big over-fat men, swinging nightsticks: tough and stupid-looking.

Keeping to the shadows, I walked along until I came to the yacht *Hermes*. It was a hundred-footer with cabin accommodation: a nice, luxury job.

I paused under the shadow of a palm tree. I could vaguely see a man sitting on the deck. The red glow of his cigarette was a splinter of light in the darkness. No lights showed in or on the yacht.

I guessed Lu Gerando was keeping guard.

I had a lot to think about. Turning, I walked back to where I had parked my car. I passed the Black Cassette. Lights showed behind the dirty, thin curtains that shielded the windows. I could hear strident dance music.

I kept on, got in my car and drove back to my home.

I spent a sleepless night, thinking of Suzy, thinking of those wonderful moments we had together, and what we had planned for the future.

At 04.00, I couldn't stand my thoughts any longer. I threw two sleeping-pills into my mouth and finally sparked out.

* * *

I walked into Glenda Kerry's office at 11.30.

'You're late, Dirk. The colonel has been asking for you.' She stared at me. 'Something wrong? You don't look well.'

'The colonel ready to see me?' I demanded curtly.

Again she stared at me, then waved to the colonel's office door.

'He's free,' she said.

Parnell was sitting at his desk. He was a giant of a man, on the wrong side of 60. His fleshy, sun-tanned face, small piercing blue eyes and the rat-trap of a mouth stamped him as a veteran soldier, and don't-let-us-forget-it.

'Morning, Dirk,' he said, regarding me as I walked into the big room with bay windows that overlooked the harbour. 'Sit down.'

I sat in a chair, facing him.

'I've read through the Thorsen file. It looked interesting, and you have done an excellent job. Well, Mrs Thorsen has pulled out, so we forget it. I've a nice job lined up for you and Anderson.'

'Not for me, Colonel,' I said quietly. 'I'm quitting.'

He lifted his big hands and let them drop on his desk.

'I was fearing you would say that, Dirk. I had hoped you could have shifted your mind to other things. I know about Suzy. I am as sorry as hell. I go along with your thinking. If I were in the unhappy position as you are, and this happened to someone I loved, I would go after those bastards.'

'That's what I am going to do,' I said.

'Right. You are suspended from work for four weeks. You will be paid as usual. Anderson can hold down your job until you return. OK?'

I shook my head.

'I appreciate this, Colonel, but I am quitting. I am going to start a war that you won't want to know about. I could even end up in the City's morgue or in jail so you must not be involved in anyway.' I got to my feet, then seeing the fat Thorsen file on his desk, I went on, 'One last favour, Colonel.' I picked up the file. 'I want this.'

81

'You think the Thorsen case has something to do with the acid job?'

'I am sure it has. Not all the facts are in this file. You don't want to know about them. Thanks, Colonel. It's been great working for you. I'm sorry it has to end this way.'

He got to his feet and thrust out his hand.

'If you get out of this mess, Dirk, you will always have a job with me.'

As I shook his hand I said, 'I don't think I will get out of this mess. I'm going to hit them where it hurts.'

'Don't do anything foolish, Dirk.'

'I'm going to hit them where it hurts, and sooner or later they will hit back. I'll let you have my resignation, and I'll tell Bill to take over the job you want fixing.'

Leaving him looking worried, I returned to my office where Bill was sitting at his desk.

We looked at each other as I sat at my desk, opposite his.

'You have my job, Bill,' I said. 'The colonel will be calling you. I am quitting.'

'That makes two of us,' Bill said quietly.

I stared at him.

'What do you mean?'

'You quit – I quit. Just that simple.'

'Why should you quit, you idiot? Look, Bill, I don't need complications. You take over, and I quit.'

'When a lovely girl like Suzy gets a face full of acid, and she's my best friend's girl,' Bill said, his voice low, 'I go with him. OK, Dirk, you may not want me, but you won't get rid of me. We quit together, and together we go after these bastards.'

'No!'

He held up his hand.

'I know. We both could land up in the morgue, but, we will have done a lot of damage by then. Write your resignation, and let me see how it is done. Then I'll write mine. Then we go back to your pad and plan a campaign.'

'No, Bill! It's terrific of you, but . . .'

'For God's sake!' Bill shouted. 'You heard me! We either work together or apart, and if I have to, I'll go after these bastards on my own.'

I stared at him, feeling an emotional surge go through me. I knew I could more than do with him. I knew as a loner I would have less chance to survive.

'Thanks,' I said. 'So, OK, we're in this together.'

I pulled my typewriter towards me and thumped out my resignation, then I ripped out the paper and gave it to Bill. He then thumped out his resignation.

'I'll go see the colonel,' he said.

'Take the two resignations with you.'

Bill came around his desk and put his hand on my shoulder.

'Between us, Dirk, we'll fix them,' he said.

'You don't know what you are walking into, Bill. Maybe we had better talk first before you see the colonel.'

'I don't give a damn what I'm walking into,' Bill said and grinned. 'I'll be back,' and he left the office.

While Bill was seeing the colonel, I cleared my desk. I had a hold-all in one of the closets, and I packed the stuff I wanted, plus the Thorsen file, plus the half finished bottle of Scotch.

When Bill returned, he gave me a wide grin.

'No problem. The colonel flipped, but he went along with my thinking. He's rooting for us, Dirk. So OK, if we both get out of this mess, our jobs will be waiting.'

'Want to clear your desk?'

'Scarcely anything to clear. I'm hungry. Let's go eat.'

'You're always hungry. Sit down. I want to talk to you.'

'Dirk, when a guy is hungry as I am, he can't concentrate. Let's go eat and talk, huh?'

I shrugged.

'OK. We'll go along and say goodbye to Glenda, then we'll go to Lucino's.'

Although it was after 19.30, Glenda was still at her desk.

'We want to say goodbye, Glenda,' I said, as Bill and I paused in the doorway.

'Come in, Dirk.' She got to her feet. 'I want to tell you how shocked and sorry I am. I want to tell you to go after these brutes. If I were in your place, I would do what you are doing.' She pushed two envelopes across the desk. 'Those are your month's salaries. Don't argue. It's the colonel's wish.'

'He's a great guy,' I said, and took the envelopes. 'Well, let's hope we'll be seeing you again.'

'Of course! One more thing, Dirk, if you want information, if you think we can be helpful, unofficially, call me. OK?'

'Thanks, Glenda.'

We all shook hands, then Bill and I walked to the elevator. I drove to Lucino's restaurant. As soon as Lucino saw me, he came rushing from behind the bar.

'Our special VIP table, Mr Wallace,' he said, shaking hands.

He led us to a table, tucked into a corner away from the other tables. At this hour there were few people waiting to be served.

As we sat down Lucino looked sorrowfully at me.

'Mr Wallace. I heard. I'm sorry. There is nothing more I can say except I grieve for you.'

I saw there were tears in his eyes. I leaned forward and patted his arm.

'Thanks,' I said. 'You are a good friend.'

'Now, Mr Wallace, I intend to prepare something very special for you. Give me the pleasure, and Mr Wallace, this is on the house. I need to express my deep-felt sympathy. Please don't say no. Leave it to me.'

I felt a wave of emotion run through me, but I controlled it.

'Thanks,' I said.

Lucino rushed away to the kitchen. I could hear him shouting to his two chefs.

84

Bill sat back.

'You certainly have good friends, Dirk,' he said. 'Man! Am I starving!'

In minutes, a waiter placed platters of stone crabs and a basket of crispy bread before us.

I knew it would be a waste of time to talk to Bill until he had taken the edge off his appetite, so we ate in silence. The waiter produced a bottle of chilled white wine and poured.

I ate little. I had too much on my mind. Food didn't interest me. When I saw Bill had finished his crab claws, I dropped half my portion onto his plate. He looked at me, nodded and dived in.

Finally, when he had finished and sat back with a sigh of content, I said, 'Can you concentrate now?'

'What's to follow?' he asked as the waiter arrived and cleared the platters.

'God knows!' I said impatiently. 'Now listen, Bill. I have been saving money, and we will need money. Neither of us will be earning anything. How are you fixed for money?'

He gave me a happy grin.

'No problem. I've stashed away twenty-five big ones. What's yours is mine, and what's mine is yours. OK?'

The waiter arrived with two more platters on which lay juicy steaks and half a lobster and a big bowl of french fries.

'Oh!' Bill exclaimed. 'Now this is like a real meal!'

We ate. A lime pie followed, then a big jug of coffee.

I refused the pie, and with growing impatience watched Bill eat.

Finally, he sat back and patted his stomach.

'The best,' he said. 'The very best!'

'Now, will you shut up and listen?' I said.

I told him what I had learned from Al Barney.

'We're going to get mixed up with the Mafia. You still have time to pull out. I must warn you this is going to be a very dangerous ride.'

Bill sipped his coffee.

'The Mafia, huh?'

'That's it.'

He nodded.

'I wondered about the acid job. It smelt to me of the Mafia. Fine. Together we take them. Just tell me what you want me to do.'

'You really mean this, Bill? We both could finish up dead. You realize this?'

For a long moment, Bill looked thoughtful, then he grinned at me and shrugged.

'So what? You can only die once. Together, we'll take them. What's the first move?'

'As we'll be working together, it would be a good idea for you to move into my spare room. Shut up your pad, and we'll be together. OK?'

Bill nodded.

'Fine with me.'

'Right. Go pack whatever you want and move in.' I put the keys of my apartment on the table. 'I'll be with you in a couple of hours.'

'What are you up to?'

'I'll tell you later. You move in. I'll be seeing you.'

I shook hands with Lucino, thanked him for the dinner, then went out into the humid night air. Getting into my car, I drove to the Thorsens' residence. As I had hoped, the place was in darkness, except for a light showing in Josh Smedley's room.

I parked the car outside the gates and walked up the drive. I had to tug the front door bell chain three times before the door was opened, and Josh gazed at me with drink-glazed eyes.

'It's Mr Wallace?' he said, peering. 'I'm sorry, Mr Wallace, Mrs Thorsen isn't in. She's at the opera. So sorry.'

I shoved my way in, sending him staggering back.

'It's you I want to see, Josh,' I said. 'It's time we talked.'

He looked defeated as only a man full of Scotch can look when faced with trouble.

'I don't think . . .' he began to mumble, but I caught his

86

arm and steered him down the corridor and into his room. There was a bottle of Scotch and a glass on the table. Josh seemed thankful to flop into his easy chair.

I sloshed more Scotch into his glass, then sat down, facing him.

'Josh, it's time you faced up to the facts,' I said, giving him my cop stare. 'Your son, Hank, is in real trouble.'

With a trembling hand, he picked up his glass, but didn't drink.

'I guess that's right, Mr Wallace.'

'Do you know he's mixed up with the Mafia?'

He made a soft moaning noise, then nodded.

'Yes, Mr Wallace. I've known it for some time. I've talked to him, but Hank is difficult. He just laughs at me. Yes, I know. He's heading for trouble.'

'No, Josh, he is not heading for trouble; he is in trouble. Do you know Angie is also mixed up with the Mafia?'

'Miss Thorsen?' He nodded and sipped his drink. 'I guess so from what I hear. She's just one of Hank's customers. I know that.'

'Blackmail customers?'

He shivered, then nodded.

'I guess that's right, but make no mistake about this, Mr Wallace, no one messes with the Mafia.'

'Why are they blackmailing Miss Thorsen?'

'I don't know. I don't want to know.'

'Hank knows?'

'I don't know. He's just a collector.'

'Mrs Thorsen hired me to find out who was blackmailing her daughter. Now, she has stopped the investigation. Do you know why?'

He took a long gulp at his drink, and for some minutes he remained still, staring with almost sightless eyes at me.

'Why?' I asked again, raising my voice.

He hesitated, then said, 'A man threatened her, Mr Wallace. I have an extension on the telephone. I heard him tell her that if she didn't call off the investigation, he would burn down her house – this house, Mr Wallace, this beautiful house.'

'Who was he?'

'Who else? The Mafia. A voice. He had that kind of voice that scares people. Mrs Thorsen listened, then hung up. I don't know anything more.'

'But you do know that Hank is heading for a fifteen-year stretch in the slammer as a blackmail collector, don't you?' I said it quietly and slowly so my words would sink in.

He flinched.

'Fifteen years?'

'That's it, Josh. Fifteen years.' Looking at this wreck of a man, I felt sorry for him.

'I've warned him,' he said, after minutes. 'He just laughs at me. What do I do, Mr Wallace? I love my son.'

'You really have no idea why Miss Thorsen is being blackmailed?'

'I'd tell you if I did. I don't know.'

'Have you any news of Terry Thorsen?'

I had to repeat the question three times before he reacted, but it was a negative reaction.

'I've heard nothing from him.'

There was no further point in staying in this sad, depressing room. I got to my feet.

'Maybe I'll be seeing you again, Josh.'

I left him, staring almost sightlessly at his half-finished drink.

In my racket you pick up all kinds of useful information.

Getting into my car, I drove down to the shabbier quarters of the waterfront where there were stalls, seedy boutiques and junk on trestle tables.

I parked and walked to a stall run by an Arab or maybe a Palestinian. I wouldn't know the difference. His name was Ali Hassan, and he sold junk to the tourists.

I found him smoking a reefer behind a stall of utter junk.

By his side, sitting on the ground, was his wife who looked like an inflated balloon about to take off.

Hassan was short, fat and wearing Arab robes with a head-dress. He looked the answer to any tourist's prayer.

'Mr Hassan,' I said, pausing before him. 'My name is Doe, I have some private business with you involving money. Can we go some place where we can talk?'

He regarded me, his little eyes like wet black olives, then he got to his feet, muttered something to his wife who shrugged her fat shoulders, then he joined me.

'Anything to do with money interests me,' he said. 'So where do we go?'

I led him to my car and got him settled in the passenger's seat. His body smell was a little overpowering and I opened all the windows. This helped, but not much.

'Mr Hassan,' I said, 'I don't want to waste your time, nor mine. I have information that you are a bomb expert. I need a bomb for which I will pay good money. Are you in the market?'

He drew on his reefer without moving his steady gaze.

'Who gave you this information?'

'Do you care? I want a bomb. If you can't deliver, just say so, and I'll shop elsewhere.'

'What kind of bomb?'

'Something small that will do a lot of damage, but won't start a fire.'

He sat silent, like a coiled fat snake, staring now at the busy waterfront, then he nodded.

'It's possible. Yes, I could arrange that, but what will you pay?'

'What's your usual charge?'

'For a small bomb, without causing fire, that is safe for an amateur to handle and will cause a lot of damage, my price would be three thousand dollars.'

He expected to haggle, and I didn't disappoint him. I spent nearly thirty minutes haggling with him. I was in no hurry. Finally, we settled for one thousand and three hundred.

89

'OK, Mr Doe,' he said. 'Tomorrow night at this time, you come to my stall and I'll deliver. No problems. A nice little job, plenty of noise, plenty of damage and no fire. OK?'

I took out my wallet and gave him five hundred. As he stowed the money away in his voluminous robes, I said, 'Mr Hassan, I know you have a good reputation. Make sure you live up to it. I could make your life a misery.'

He grinned uneasily.

'No problems, Mr Doe.'

He climbed out of my car and went waddling back through the stream of tourists to his junk stall.

I set the air-conditioner working to clear his smell, then closed the windows and headed for home.

As I drove through the traffic-congested streets, I thought that in the early hours of tomorrow morning the Black Cassette would no longer be in business.

So, OK, this was revenge, but whatever I did wouldn't bring Suzy's bright face again on my pillow.

6

It was just after 23.00 when I rang on my front-door bell.
There was a delay as Bill regarded me through the spy-hole,
then he opened up.

'No problems, Bill?' I asked, as he re-locked the front
door.

'I've settled in.' He moved into the living-room. On the
table was the Thorsen file. 'I've been going over this, Dirk,
over and over, because pretty soon we've got to squeeze
something out of it. Something or somebody's got to give.'

I sank into an easy chair.

'Let me shoot off my mouth, Bill,' I said, then went on to
tell him about my talk with Josh Smedley.

'The Mafia are active,' I concluded. 'Well, OK. We
expected this. They've put the fear of God into Mrs
Thorsen. No news of Terry.' I paused to light a cigarette.
'Now, Hank. I intend to make his life a misery.' I went on
to tell Bill about the bomb. 'It'll wreck his club. I am going
to wreck his car. I want him to feel life is on top of him.
Then I'm going to wreck his home. Now, Bill, the big point
is I don't want Hank to get the idea that it is me after him. If
he does, he'll run to his Mafia pals and scream for protection, and we could be in trouble.'

I got to my feet and went into the kitchen. I found a small
piece of cardboard. On it I wrote with a felt pen the
following:

BLACKS NOT WANTED HERE: K.K.K.

I returned to the living-room and showed Bill the notice.

'This will be tacked on the door of the club. It should
divert Hank's thinking that it is me after him. I'll do the

same with the car. This way we'll gain some breathing-space.'

'I see that,' Bill said, nodding.

'Of course, sooner or later, the Mafia thugs will realize it is me hitting them, and then they'll hit back. We have to be ready for that. So once we really get started, we must go underground. I know a place where we can live. It'll mean leaving here. OK with you, Bill?'

'If you say so, it's fine with me.'

I got to my feet.

'I'm going to bed. You keep out of this bomb job, Bill. I'm doing this on my own.'

'Not a chance,' Bill said. 'Where you go, I go too. OK, let's go to bed.'

'I don't want you. This is a one-man job.'

'Two men are always better than one,' Bill said and went off to his bedroom.

I had a quick shower, then got into bed. I put my hand on the empty pillow where Suzy's lovely head so often rested. I thought of her getting acid sprayed in her face, her awful pain and rushing into the street where that truck smashed her to pieces. I didn't sleep that night. I lay and thought of those times we had had together, how she had done so much for me, added so much richness to my life.

It wasn't until the sun began to come through the rain-cloudy sky, that I finally fell asleep, but only for an hour. I dreamed of Hank, this massive ape of a man, and I woke up, sweating, and seeing the time, I got up, shaved, showered and dressed.

Bill was already up. He had coffee on the table and rounds of toast and jam. We sat opposite each other.

We ate in silence for several minutes, then he said, 'OK, Dirk, when you have fixed Hank, what's the next move?'

I shook my head.

'I don't know. I've got this slob on my mind, and I can't think of anything else.'

'I can understand that,' he said, 'but isn't there something I can do?'

'God knows!' I said impatiently. 'You joined me. You'll have to put up with me!'

Bill finished his coffee.

'OK. So I'll go out and take a look at the scene. Let's have lunch here. What are you going to do?'

'I'll be waiting for tonight,' I said, shoving my coffee-cup away from me. 'You do what you like.'

'Can I take the car?'

'Oh, sure. I'll be here. I have nothing to do, but to wait until that dump of his closes at 3 A.M.'

'Try and take it easy, Dirk.' Then getting to his feet, he left the apartment.

I took time washing the coffee-cups and clearing the table. I moved like a zombie. I was like a man with an inflamed, festering boil that had to be lanced. The boil was Hank Smedley. I sat in the living-room, smoking cigarette after cigarette, and thinking always of Suzy. The hours dragged. It wasn't until 13.00 that Bill returned.

'I've got two steaks,' he said, and went into the kitchen.

Food didn't interest me. I heard the grill sizzling. I lit another cigarette.

Bill came in, laid the table and dished up the steaks. We ate them with coarse brown bread. I played with my food. My mind was too obsessed with Suzy and Hank.

'I went down to the waterfront,' Bill said as he finished his steak. 'I talked around. Hank's club shuts at two thirty. Everyone leaves. The place will be deserted.'

'Nice work, Bill,' I said, pushing my half-finished steak from me. 'Fine. I'll go down there at two and case the joint. I've got to get in, and there are those two waterfront cops to watch out for.'

'We'll go down there, Dirk,' Bill said firmly.

I shrugged.

'If you want to. Yes, OK, you will be helpful.'

93

'Jesus!' Bill exclaimed, staring at me. 'You are in a mental mess, aren't you?'

'I've got to fix this black bastard. I want to kill him, but I'm not starting on murder. So, I'll make his life a misery.'

'I know. You told me. You are going to blow the Black Cassette to hell. Fine. So, when you have made Hank's life a misery, what are you going to do?'

'There's time to think about that,' I said. 'See you, Bill,' and I left the apartment.

Soft rain was falling. I walked, not noticing the rain. I walked for hours. The streets of Paradise City were almost deserted. As I walked my thoughts churned with pictures of Suzy and Hank. I kept seeing in my mind Suzy leaving her apartment block: a car stopping, a request for directions, then the acid. Some thug had handled the acid. Hank had driven the car.

I paused outside police headquarters, hesitated, then went in. I asked to speak to Sergeant Joe Beigler. Charlie Tanner, the desk sergeant, regarded me with sympathy.

'I'm sorry, Dirk, about your trouble,' he said. 'Go right on up. Joe'll see you.'

Beigler heaved himself out of his desk chair and gave me a double-fisted handshake. He was trying to express sympathy. I needed sympathy like lemon juice on an open wound.

'Any news, Joe?' I asked, putting my hands on his desk and leaning forward.

'A little – not much,' Beigler said, dropping back into his chair. 'We came on a witness who lives in a condo above where it happened. He saw the whole thing, and got the number of the car – stolen. Both men wore gloves – no fingerprints. The driver was black. That's as far as we've got, but we're still investigating.'

'He's sure the driver was black?'

'He swears to that.'

'If that's the best you can do, I won't waste your time.'

94

Turning, I left him and walked out into the drizzle of rain. At least, I was now certain that Hank was involved.

I walked down a side-street and arrived on the waterfront. After a couple of minutes, I slowed my pace as I came upon the Black Cassette. Outside the place was the Olds that once had belonged to Terry Thorsen: a nice car. I moved more slowly. The time now was 16.30. Hank would be preparing for the evening's shindig. I kept on and took a a long look at Joe Walinski's luxury yacht. As there were other tourists, done up in their plastic macs, also staring at the yacht, I paused and joined them.

The man I knew as Lu Gerando was pacing the deck. He stared down at the tourists and sneered at them. After Hank, I thought, this yacht would go. I would have to have a limpet mine. Ali Hassan would supply that. He would supply anything if the money was big enough.

I had walked far enough. I took a taxi home.

Bill was out. I had more hours to kill. I sat down and forced myself to relax. Action tonight, I kept thinking. Hitting back.

Bill returned soon after 20.00. I let him in and he was carrying a plastic sack in one hand and a duffel bag in the other.

'Let's eat,' he said, dropping the two bags. 'I'm starving.'

He went into the kitchen, and I returned to my chair. I wasn't hungry: only hungry for revenge.

A few minutes later, Bill appeared with hamburgers, heated up. He set the table and sat down.

'Come on, Dirk, for God's sake!' he said sharply. 'You'll be a nut-case if you don't watch out.'

I picked at the hamburger.

'Where have you been?'

'Around and about. Now, look, Dirk, let's get Hank fixed first. Maybe, when we've fixed him, you'll be able to listen and make some sense. OK?'

'What's in the duffel bag?'

'All we'll need to break into Hank's club, and all we'll need to smash up his car.'

I nodded and suddenly found I was hungry. I ate the hamburger.

'I've talked to Beigler. The cops are getting nowhere, but they have found a witness who swears the driver was black.'

'We more or less knew that,' Bill said, his mouth full. He darted into the kitchen and came back with two more hamburgers. We ate them, and I kept looking at my watch. The time now was 20.35. God! I thought, how time drags!

I went back to my chair, lit a cigarette while Bill cleared the table. I was tempted to have a double Scotch, but refrained. This wasn't the time to get reckless on Scotch.

Finally at 21.00, I got to my feet.

'I'll get the bomb, Bill.'

'Fine. I'll come along. I've got nothing to do.'

Leaving Bill sitting in the parked car, I walked to Ali Hassan's junk stall. In spite of the drizzle the tourists were still on the waterfront, most of them staring at the junk stalls. It was several minutes before Hassan, sitting under an awning, saw me. He got to his feet, spoke to his wife, then joined me.

'You got it?' I asked.

'Yes. It's a beautiful job, Mr Doe. Worth every dollar you are paying for it.'

'Let me have it, and I'll give you the money.'

'That's as it should be. It is all ready. Now listen, Mr Doe, there is no problem. There is a switch at the top. You turn that to the right and the bomb goes off in ten minutes. It is safe so long as you don't touch the switch. You can even drop it. No problem.'

Moving into the deeper shadows, I took out my wallet and gave him the balance of the money we had agreed on. He counted the money, nodded and stowed the bills under his robe.

'Just a minute, Mr Doe.' He waddled away, then returned carrying a plastic sack. This he gave me. 'Turn the switch to the right, Mr Doe, then take off. In ten minutes there will be a big bang and a lot of damage.'

'Could be I will want something else,' I said. 'Something that could sink a hundred-foot yacht. You in the market?'

He put his hand under his robe and scratched himself.

'That would come expensive, Mr Doe. I could arrange it, but I would have to fix it with a Marine sergeant who comes very high.'

'But you could arrange it?'

'If the money is right, anything can be arranged.'

'I could be seeing you again,' I said, and leaving him, I returned to the car. I put the plastic sack on the back seat and slid under the driving wheel.

'That it?' Bill asked, turning to stare at the sack.

'That's it.' I started the motor. 'We'll go home and wait.'

'I'm not crazy about bombs,' Bill said. 'Is that thing safe?'

'It's OK,' I told him. 'Relax,' and I drove back to my condominium. In the underground garage, I opened the plastic sack and took from it a black, square-shaped object. As Hassan had said, there was a small switch on the top of the box. Bill watched, his eyes goggling.

'You push this switch to the right,' I said, 'and after ten minutes – boom!' I returned the bomb to the sack, and leaving the car, we took the elevator up to my apartment.

'We have a five-hour wait,' I said. 'Let's have some coffee.'

'Sure.' Bill went into the kitchen.

I put the bomb on the table, then, lighting a cigarette, I sat down.

Bill came in with a jug of coffee, a cup and saucer.

'I'm taking a nap, Dirk. Call me when you are ready to take off.'

When he had gone to his bedroom, I drank coffee, smoked cigarettes, paced the living-room, constantly looking at my watch. My mind now was solely on the thought of making Hank Smedley's life miserable as he had made my life miserable.

Finally, at 01.45, I roused Bill who was sleeping peacefully. I envied him.

'Let's go,' I said. 'We'll take a look at the scene.'

So with the plastic sack containing the bomb and the KKK notice, we drove down to the waterfront. It had begun to rain again. The waterfront was more or less deserted. A few fishermen were leaving their boats. The tourists were in bed. There was no sign of the two waterfront cops.

I found easy parking within a hundred yards of the Black Cassette.

'I'll take a look, Bill,' I said, and slid out of the car.

Leaving him, I walked past the club, hearing jazz. There was a side alley that I guessed led to the back of the club. Moving silently, I went down the alley and peered into a rear window of the club. It was a window which would offer no resistance. I saw a couple of blacks wandering around. The room looked like a makeshift kitchen.

One of the blacks was taking off his dirty apron as if preparing to go home. The other sat on a table, munching a hot dog.

I ducked away, then moved silently back to the car. I joined Bill.

'There's a rear window. No problem,' I said.

We sat in silence and waited. By now the waterfront was quite deserted. Rain fell steadily. The only lights showing came from the Black Cassette.

As the hands of my watch crawled to 02.30, some of the lights in the club went out. There was a babble of voices, then some thirty-odd blacks, men and women, came out onto the sidewalk. They were all chattering like magpies. After a minute or so the group broke up. There was a lot of shouting and waving, and they dispersed down the various alleys.

Then four big black men, who I guessed were the staff,

came out and hurried to a car parked not far from where we were parked. They scrambled in and drove away.

Just after 03.00, Hank Smedley appeared. There was no mistaking his giant, ape-like figure. He and a man wearing a wide-brimmed hat and a white jacket paused for a moment while Hank locked the door of the club. Then they walked rapidly to Hank's Olds, got in and drove away.

'Who's the guy wearing the hat?' Bill asked. 'He's white.'

'I don't know and I don't care,' I said. 'Come on, Bill, we have a job to do.'

We left the car. Bill had taken a short jemmy from the duffel bag. I carried the bomb.

It took Bill less than a minute to open the window into the smelly kitchen. I had brought a powerful flashlight with me. I switched it on, then motioned Bill to give me the bomb. 'I'll fix this. You go and fix the KKK notice on the door.'

I found my way into the big room where the blacks danced. I put the bomb on the bar counter. Then, gun in hand, I checked the whole place to be sure no one was sleeping there – no one was.

Satisfied, I returned to the bar and pushed the switch on the bomb to the right. Then I returned fast to the kitchen, climbed through the window and joined Bill in the car.

'Think we are far enough away?' Bill asked, an anxious note in his voice.

'I want to see it,' I said, gripping the steering-wheel, my eyes on the club, thinking this was the first step towards avenging Suzy, and I felt good.

The hands of the car's dashboard clock crawled on. Ten minutes passed.

Bill moved uneasily.

'It could be a goddamn dud!' he muttered as the hands of the clock reached fifteen minutes past.

'Quiet! Wait!' I snapped.

I had scarcely stopped speaking when the bomb exploded. The noise and the blast rocked us and rocked the car.

The front windows of the club flew onto the waterfront.

There was a tearing sound as the club's roof collapsed. I saw the front door sagging, holding the KKK notice. There was more noise: more sound of the club falling apart.

This was good enough for me. I started the car's motor and drove off the waterfront before the cops and firemen arrived.

I had done what I wanted to do. The Back Cassette was permanently out of business. The realization of this was like a great weight lifted off my back.

'Some bomb,' Bill said. 'Now what?'

'You know where Hank lives?'

'Sure.'

'So we go there and wreck his car.'

He directed me to Seagrove Road.

'That's his pad. On the right.'

I parked, then both of us, armed with short-handled club hammers, walked down to the underground garage.

It took us less than ten minutes to reduce Hank's car to scrap. While I smashed the window and windscreen, Bill fixed the engine. There was noise, but at 04.15, who paid attention to noise? We stabbed the tyres, then using my felt pencil I wrote on the only undented door panel: KKK.

Then we retreated to my car.

'Satisfied?' Bill asked as I started the motor.

'Yes,' I said. 'I'll sleep. Thanks, Bill.'

I headed back to my apartment.

For the first time since Suzy died, I slept dreamlessly. By the time I got out of bed, shaved, showered and dressed, it was 11.15.

Bill had a brunch ready, and while we ate he regarded me searchingly.

'I think you are over the hump, Dirk,' he said, cutting into his third egg.

'I guess so,' I said. 'Hank drove the car, but I've got to find the acid sprayer. I've got to fix him too.'

'So, OK, we'll fix him,' Bill said. 'We'll ask around.'

After the meal I drove with Bill to the waterfront. Parking was tight, but finally I found a slot, then together we walked by the junk stalls, the fishing trawlers and finally reached what remained of the Black Cassette.

There was a crowd of tourists, gaping. They were held back by the two waterfront cops. I spotted Detective Tom Lepski talking to a fireman.

'Stay here,' I said to Bill, and shoved my way through the crowd.

One of the waterfront cops started towards me.

'Hi, Tom!' I called, then as Lepski waved to me the cop pulled back. I joined Lepski.

'Take a look,' he said, waving to the broken entrace of the club. 'Something for the record.'

I had a hard time to conceal my satisfaction as I peered through the sagging doorway. The bomb had done a great job.

'Looks like a bomb,' I said.

'Damn right. Something that's never happened in this city. The mayor is laying eggs.' Lepski grinned. 'It was time someone fixed this club. Well, whoever it was, certainly fixed it.'

'I guess that's right,' I said, aware Lepski was regarding me thoughtfully.

'Yeah. There's a Ku-Klux-Klan notice on the door, but that doesn't wash with me nor anyone else. Someone who hated Smedley did the job,' Lepski said.

I nodded.

'You may be right, Tom. Have you seen Smedley?'

'Oh, sure.' Lepski shrugged. 'I've got no time for that spade. Someone smashed up his car. We reckon it's the same guy who let off the bomb. Smedley is out of his mind, yelling for us to find the guy.' He shrugged. 'OK, it's our job to look around, but we're not going to sweat. Smedley had it coming.' Again the hard cop stare. 'I hear you have quit the agency, Dirk.'

'That's right. Suzy's death has taken the stuffing out of

me. Maybe, I'll return to the agency in time. How are your investigations getting on about Suzy, Tom?'

'We're still digging. We've found another witness, and from her, we have a description of the guy who used the acid: not much of a description, but maybe it'll help. He was broad-shouldered, wearing a white jacket and a broad-brimmed hat. We are looking for someone to match that description.'

My face expressionless, I nodded.

I remembered the man who had come out with Hank from the club, wearing a white jacket and a broad-brimmed hat. They had gone off together.

Lepski was still regarding me.

'Look, Dirk, Hank's been fixed. We don't want any more trouble. This is a very sensitive zone. The news is being broadcast that a bomb has gone off. Bombs scare the rich to hell. Already hotels are getting cancellations for next month. We don't want any more bombs. You read me, Dirk?'

'Why tell me, Tom? You'd better tell the bomber if he will listen.'

Lepski shrugged.

'Play it your way,' he said, 'but I'm telling you if another bomb goes off, we'll throw the book at the bomber. He'll go away for fifteen years.'

'You tell him that,' I said. 'Well, be seeing you, Tom,' and I moved back into the crowd.

I signalled to Bill to stay where he was, then walked along the waterfront to the Neptune Tavern. I found Al Barney, sitting on his bollard, talking to two young, goggle-eyed tourists. I waited. Finally they took photographs of him, and the man produced a ten-dollar bill. Al snapped it up, waved to them as they walked away.

'Tourist trade prospering, Al?' I said as I came up to him.

'Ah, Mr Wallace. Well, it comes and it goes.' He put the bill in his dirty sweat-shirt pocket. 'Next month will be the time.' He regarded me with his small shark-like eyes. 'Some bomb,' he went on. 'That puts paid to Smedley.'

102

'Al, do you know anything about a broad-shouldered man who wears a white jacket and a wide-brimmed hat?'

Barney grimaced.

'Hula Minsky,' he said. 'Keep clear of him, Mr Wallace.'

'Who is he?'

Barney looked furtively around then, lowering his voice, said, 'One of Walinski's thugs. Poison.'

'Where do I find him?'

'You don't want to find him, Mr Wallace. Like I said – poison.'

'Where do I find him, Al?' I repeated.

Barney moaned.

'When he's here, he shacks up with Hank Smedley. He comes down here before the first of the month to collect the pay-offs.'

'Thanks, Al,' I said, and giving him a pat on his fat shoulder, I walked back to where Bill was waiting.

'The cops are pretty sure I let off the bomb,' I concluded after telling him what I had been doing. 'Lepski gave me a straight warning, but they have no proof.'

Bill shrugged.

'The cops always have theories.' He slid into the passenger's seat. 'Hula Minsky – some name. What are you going to do with him?'

'Bust him. I'm going to bust him so hard, he'll go around in a wheelchair for life.' I started the car motor.

'When?'

'Tonight. Around seven, we'll stake out Hank's apartment and wait.'

'That could be tough.'

'So, OK, it'll be tough.'

'You handle Minsky. I'll handle Hank,' Bill said. 'I'm thirsting to hit that black.'

'That's the idea, Bill.'

Back in my apartment, Bill moved around the living-room restlessly while I lit a cigarette and brooded.

The telephone bell rang. I reached and picked up the receiver.

'Mr Wallace?' A woman's voice.

'Correct. Who is this?'

'I am Mr Walinski's secretary,' the voice told me: a hard, metallic voice of a woman who could be of any age. 'Mr Walinski would like to talk to you. Will you come to the Spanish Bay Hotel at five o'clock. I will be waiting for you in the lobby and will take you to Mr Walinski's suite.'

The phone clicked off before I could say a word. I put down the receiver and told Bill.

Bill whistled softly. We both knew that the Spanish Bay Hotel was the best, most expensive and most exclusive hotel on the east coast.

'Does himself well. Are you going?'

'I'm going,' I said.

At a few minutes to five o'clock, I walked into the ornate lobby of the Spanish Bay Hotel.

There was the usual scene: old residents sitting, drinking tea and yakking. This was a place for only the rich. Two waiters moved around, pushing trolleys loaded with cream buns and fancy cakes. They were not short of customers.

She was waiting by the reception desk: tall, raven-black hair, green eyes: not a beauty, but so sensual, her vibes seemed to flick out of her like sparks. She was in white: a short coat and a beautifully tailored skirt. She looked a million dollars.

She lifted a hand with long, slender fingers and came towards me.

'Mr Wallace? I am Sandra. My other name doesn't matter. I'm always known as Sandra.'

'Hi, Sandra,' I said, looking at her body. She had everything a man could desire. Big breasts, tiny waist, solid buttocks and long legs. 'What's all this about?'

'Mr Walinski wants to talk to you. Be careful with him, Mr Wallace.' She regarded me thoughtfully. 'He's not what he appears,' then, turning, she led the way to the bank of elevators. We rode up to the sixth floor and walked down a long passage, then she paused at a door, inserted a key, then paused to look at me.

'Be careful,' she murmured, and opening the door, she stood aside and waved me into a big room with a vast terrace. It was all very de luxe.

I walked in.

'Mr Walinski, Mr Wallace is here,' Sandra said, raising her voice. 'He's on the terrace,' she said to me.

So I walked across the big room and out onto the terrace that overlooked the beach, the palm trees, the bathers and the sea.

Joe Walinski was standing by the balcony rail. He turned and came towards me.

I was surprised. I was expecting to see a big, threatening thug of a man. Knowing that Walinski was a mafioso, knowing he was a blackmailer, I was thrown off balance by his appearance.

Smiling, was a short, thickset man who could be any one of the many big-shot businessmen one sees down here on vacation. He was slightly overweight, balding, sun-tanned, immaculately dressed in a lightweight pale blue suit, a silk cream-coloured shirt, and some kind of club tie, his feet in Gucci slip-ons.

His round well-fed face was equipped with a short nose, a wide, almost lipless mouth and blue-grey eyes, set wide apart. He had a big dimple in his jutting chin. He oozed wealth and good humour.

'Good of you to come, Mr Wallace,' he said, offering his hand.

I hesitated, then shook hands. He had a firm but not aggressive grip.

'Let's sit down. It looks as if we're going to have more rain. This is the rainy season.' He led the way to a table and chairs, covered with an awning, and waved me to one of the chairs.

We sat down, and I was aware he was sizing me up.

Those blue-grey eyes were searching: eyes that never missed a thing.

'Coffee, perhaps?' he said. 'It is a little early for a drink.'

'Nothing, thank you.'

'Perhaps tea?'

'Nothing, thanks.'

He lifted his heavy shoulders.

'Well then, let us talk. I am busy. You are busy. We mustn't waste each other's time.'

I waited.

He crossed one short leg over the other.

'I want to tell you how sincerely sorry I am about Miss Suzy Long. I want you to believe that this devilish job was done without my knowledge. This was done by a man who happens to work for me. He was a mindless creature who would do anything for money. When I questioned him, he confessed he had received five thousand dollars to do this devilish job. He told me he had got the money from Hank Smedley who was acting for someone else. He didn't know who. Under pressure, he said it was a private vendetta.'

I was listening. My mind switched back to the scene in the bank when Angela Thorsen had hissed at me: *'I will make you sorry for this! God! You will be sorry!'* I saw again her frustrated expression. Was it she who had given Hank five thousand dollars to ruin Suzy's face?

'Mr Wallace, you have settled accounts with Smedley. I have settled accounts with my man.' Walinski paused and those grey-blue eyes suddenly became steel-blue eyes. 'He is a thing of the past. I have an organization that takes care of people like him: no fuss: finish. As for Smedley, I no longer employ him. If it will make you feel better, he too, can be a thing of the past. Would that please you?'

'You mean you turn your thumb down and Hank will be dead?' I said.

'That's crudely put, Mr Wallace, but not to waste time, just tell me.'

'Let him live.'

'You have a forgiving nature, Mr Wallace. If someone had done to my girl what those two did to yours, I wouldn't be forgiving.'

'Let him live,' I said. 'I will make his life a misery.'

He nodded.

'I am sure you will.'

Sandra came out with a tray of coffee things, set the tray on the table, poured two cups of black coffee and then went away.

She was so electrifyingly sensual, I had to make a considerable effort not to turn in my chair and watch her cross the terrace.

I became aware Walinski was watching me.

'She's a useful girl,' he said with his good-humoured smile. 'Her father once worked for me. When he died, I took her on as my secretary. She is quite indispensable now.'

I said nothing.

He slipped his coffee. I didn't touch mine.

'Well now, Mr Wallace, let us conclude this meeting,' he said. 'I hope you are satisfied. I want you to be satisfied. My man is no more. I leave Smedley's future in your hands. Now, Mr Wallace, I realize that by destroying Smedley's club you took a quick revenge. However, when a bomb goes off in this tranquil city, it causes a ripple of fear among the rich who come here. I don't want any more bombs. My business is with the rich. If they think there will be more bombs, they will go elsewhere, and that's bad for my business. You are an intelligent man. You will understand what I am saying, but at the same time, you could be tempted to start more trouble. I ask you not to do that.' He smiled. I was beginning to hate his wide, good-humoured smile. To me, it was like a rattlesnake smiling. 'As you probably know, I am part of a vast organization which operates in every country in the world.' He finished his coffee and set down his cup. 'So I advise you not to cause any more trouble in this city. But if you do, you will regret the impulse. Is that understood?'

107

I got to my feet.

'I hear you, Mr Walinski,' and turning, I walked across the terrace and into the big living-room.

Sandra was waiting and moved to the door. She paused, her hand on the door handle, and we looked at each other. No woman I had ever seen compared to her. She wasn't a woman I could love as I had loved Suzy. She was apart from all other women I had known. Those green eyes were compelling: dangerous, fascinating eyes. Then there was her sensuality, her body, and the complete, cold confidence so few women have.

She opened the door, and as I moved by her she said in a whisper, 'Tonight. Eleven o'clock. The Three Crab Restaurant.'

For a moment, I didn't believe what she had said. I turned, but the door had shut in my face.

I returned to my apartment just after 18.00.

Bill was at my desk, still reading the Thorsen file. He left it reluctantly and joined me in a lounging chair with a stiff Scotch I made.

In detail, I told him of my interview with Walinski. He listened.

'It seems to me, Bill, this wasn't the Mafia, but a private vendetta job, carried out by Hank and Minsky for five thousand dollars. Minsky is buried somewhere where he won't be found, so we don't have to worry about him. Now, Hank . . .'

'Yes, Hank,' Bill said nodding.

'We're going to call on him, and we are going to find out who hired him to do this acid job. I can guess it was Angela Thorsen, but I want to know for sure. When he sings, and if it is Angela, then we go after her.'

Again Bill nodded.

'How do we make a big ape like Hank sing?'

'Can you put your hands on a blowtorch?'

Bill grinned.

'Oh, sure. Yes, that's a good idea. We burn him a little, then he sings.'

He brooded while he finished his drink.

'How did Walinski strike you, Dirk?'

'Dangerous: a snake. Not anyone to fool with.' I went on to tell him about Sandra. He listened, pop-eyed.

'You meeting her?' he asked.

'Why not? Know anything about the Three Crab?'

Bill was always a mine of information about restaurants and clubs.

'On the waterfront. Good. Expensive. Next to Solly Joel's joint. You know that?'

'Right. OK, Bill, see what you can do about a blowtorch. I'll talk to Hank on the telephone.'

'The janitor is certain to have one.' He left the apartment, and I went to a closet and dug out two pairs of handcuffs. I got my .38 from its box, checked it was loaded and dropped it into my pocket. Then I got the telephone book and looked up Hank's number.

It took over a dozen rings before Hank snarled, 'Who is it?'

'Mr Smedley?' I made my voice sound tough and hard. 'This is police headquarters.'

'Oh, yeah? So what? You found that fucker who bombed out my joint?'

'That's what we want to talk to you about, Mr Smedley. Just a few questions. We are sending two detectives around to your place. OK?'

'Yeah. Hurry it up. I've got to go out in an hour,' and he hung up.

Bill returned, carrying a blowtorch.

'No problem. It's new and works well,' he said.

'Right. Then let's go.'

'Look, Dirk, I want to take care of this ape. Will you give me the front seat?'

'You're just thirsting to see if your Sunday punch settles him.'

109

'It will.'

We reached Seagrove Road in ten minutes. We rode up to the top floor.

'This is for me,' Bill said.

I stood aside, leaning against the wall, gun in hand. I watched Bill as he thumbed the bell-push.

There was a pause, then the door jerked open. Hank stood there. He was wearing tight-fitting jeans. The upper part of his body was naked. As he stood glaring down at Bill, I don't think I've seen a finer-built body of muscle apart from professional boxers.

'You a cop?' Hank snarled, then he stiffened. 'I know you! Goddamn it! Get the hell out of here before I smear you!'

Bill said something in a low voice which Hank couldn't hear. He did what Bill wanted him to do. He leaned forward, thrusting his ape-like face at Bill. He made a perfect target. Bill's fist, protected by his knuckle-duster, slammed against Hank's jaw with a 'thwack' that made me wince.

Hank's eyes rolled back, showing only the whites, and he went down like a pole-axed bull.

'Spaghetti,' Bill said contemptuously.

Together, we dragged the huge body into the living-room. It took me only a few seconds to handcuff the thick wrists behind his muscular back, then handcuff his ankles together.

Bill shut and locked the front door. We paused to look around.

At one time, the living-room was comfortable and well furnished, but now it was showing shabbiness and neglect. I went, gun in hand into the two bedrooms and the tiny kitchen, which was in a mess, and then checked out the bathroom, also messy. Hank was on his own.

'OK, Bill, don't let's waste time on this jerk,' I said. 'Get some water and get him to the surface.'

Bill went into the kitchen, found a bucket, half filled it

with water and sloshed the water in Hank's unconscious face. He then pumped up the blowtorch and got it going. There was a hiss, and a blue-yellow flame came through the vent holes.

Hank stirred, opened his eyes, shook his head, moaned and closed his eyes. I kicked him solidly in the ribs, making him groan as he struggled to sit up. With my foot on his forehead, I slammed him back on the soaking wet carpet.

He snarled at me the way a jungle cat, trapped, will snarl at the hunter.

'Who paid you five thousand to acid-job my girl?' I demanded.

He wrestled with the handcuffs, but that got him nowhere. They were the kind that became tighter the more you wrestled.

'Don't know what you're talking about,' he mumbled.

I looked at Bill.

'Let him have a flick of heat,' I said.

'My pleasure,' Bill said and ran the blue-yellow flame with a quick motion over Hank's naked chest. Hank screamed. He seemed to fall to pieces. The snarl and the hate went. Now deep fear took over.

'Don't do it!' he gasped. 'OK, I'll tell you. Just don't do that again.'

'Who?' I demanded, squatting by his side.

'Angie. Keep that flame away from me!'

'Tell me!'

Bill moved forward and waved the hissing flame near Hank's face. He squealed. Sweat poured off him.

'Tell me!' I shouted at him.

'Angie came to me. She was crazy mad that you stopped her getting Terry's money. Crazy mad! I'm telling you! She scared me! It was her idea about the acid. When she offered five big ones, I talked to Hula who arranges anything. So we did it. I didn't mean for her to get killed. I swear I didn't. I thought it would be a little bit of skin

111

peeling. I swear I didn't think she would run into the road and get smashed up by a truck. I swear it!'

I looked at him with loathing.

'Did you get the money?'

'Sure thing. When Angie says she'll pay, she pays. I got half. Hula got the other half.'

'Where's Hula?'

'I dunno. He had a call last night. He said he had to go out on business. He hasn't come back.'

'Did he say where he was going?'

'I don't ask Hula questions,' Hank said, eyeing the blowtorch. 'No one in their right skulls asks Hula questions. I dunno where he is.'

I could have told him, but decided not to.

'OK, Hank, we're making progress,' I said. 'Now Angie. She's been paying you ten thousand a month, hasn't she?'

He shook his head as Bill shifted the flame of the blowlamp.

'Not to me. Look, this is how it works. Hula comes to me. He wants to use my club as a drop. He pays me five hundred a week to use my club. So, OK, I go along with that. He owns this pad. He lets me use it. I don't know a thing. I swear it!'

'Keep talking,' I said.

Bill moved a little closer so Hank could feel the heat of the flame. He cringed away.

'People come to my club and give me envelopes. Angie gives me a wallet. I put everything in a bag. I don't ask questions. On the first of the month, Hula comes and I give him the bag, and that's it.'

'Why is Angie being blackmailed?'

'I dunno. I swear I don't! It's Hula who digs up the dirt about people. I don't ask questions. I don't want to know. I guess Hula has something on Angie. Something so hot, she is paying out all this dough. She ain't right in the head. She's a real nut-case. She's always been a nut-case.'

I studied him and decided he was telling the truth. A

112

brutal, ruthless man like Minsky wouldn't tell a bird-brain like Hank anything.

I was suddenly sick of him, sick of the room, sick of the atmosphere.

'OK, Bill,' I said. 'Unlock him.'

Bill turned off the blowtorch, then removed the handcuffs while I, gun in hand, watched.

Hank sat up, rubbed his wrists and stared up at me.

'Listen carefully,' I said. 'there's no place now for you in this city. I talked to Hula's boss. Hula's feeding the worms. You won't see him again, and I don't want to see you again. You have twelve hours to get out of this city. If I see you again, you will get a bullet in each kneecap and you won't be able to walk again. Get lost! Understand?'

He continued to stare, shaking his head in bewilderment.

'I don't know where to go,' he muttered. 'I ain't got any money.'

'I won't tell you twice. If you're not out of this city in twelve hours, you won't walk again.' I turned. 'Come on, Bill. The sight of this shit sickens me.'

We took the elevator down to the street level and walked out into the humid rain.

7

From the outside, the Three Crab Restaurant didn't look inspiring. It had a tatty, weather-beaten air with its bleached wooden front and its narrow glass door, screened by a red curtain: not an enticement to tourists.

When I pushed open the door, I found myself in a tiny lobby with a Vietnamese acting as a hat-check girl. She gave me a welcoming smile.

'You have a reservation, sir?' she asked.

'I am expected.'

'Would you be Mr Wallace?'

'That's right.'

She pressed a bell-push on the counter.

'Just one moment, sir.'

A short, fat man, wearing a grey alpaca coat, white shirt with a string tie and black trousers, materialized.

'Mr Wallace?'

'Correct,' I said.

'Miss Sandra Willis is expecting you, Mr Wallace.' I got a flashing smile, revealing white capped teeth. 'Please to follow me.'

He opened a door, and the sound of voices, the clatter of dishes, startled me. I followed him into a vast room, crowded with tables and packed with people. Some of the men wore white tuxedos. All the women were dressed to kill. Waiters were moving swiftly and efficiently, changing plates, serving dishes.

'You have quite a business here,' I said as he led me by a packed bar and to a flight of stairs.

He turned and gave me his flashing, toothy smile.

'I don't complain.'

114

He led me up the stairs, reached a door, tapped and threw the door open, bowing me in.

'Mr Wallace, Miss Willis.'

She was sitting at a table, laid for dinner in a small, but well furnished, air-conditioned room. She waved to me and motioned me to sit at the table. She was wearing a dark red dress, and her black hair was caught back by a band of pearls. She looked terrific, and I caught her sexual vibes as I sat, facing her.

'Let's eat, Wally,' she said. 'I'm starving.'

'Two seconds, Miss Willis,' the man in the alpaca coat said and vanished.

She regarded me.

'I need to talk to you,' she said, 'but first I must eat. I haven't had a thing since last night. J.W. is very exacting.'

'J.W.? Walinski?'

'Who else?'

There was a tap on the door, and a waiter who looked Mexican hurried in. He put a plate of a dozen oysters Rockefeller before Sandra and the same for me. He then poured a chilled white wine and, bowing, he left us.

The oysters were excellent. As I speared my fifth I said, 'You seem at home here, Sandra.'

'I come here most nights. When a woman is usually on her own, it is wise to eat privately, and where she is known.'

'I shouldn't have thought you were often alone.'

She shrugged.

'My working hours are impossible. It is only that J.W. decided to go to the casino, I am eating now.'

'You want to talk to me?'

'Yes, but not yet.'

By now we had finished the oysters and I heard a bell ring. I guessed she had pressed a hidden bell-push on the floor.

Almost immediately, the waiter appeared and cleared the plates, then yet another waiter appeared, pushing a hotplate trolley.

'You don't object to seafood?' she asked me.

'I don't object to any food.'

The waiter served from a big dish. He placed before Sandra half a grilled shelled lobster, fried clams and king-sized prawns, stuffed with crab meat. He served rice with a scattering of red peppers over which he poured a thick, creamy sauce tinted pink by lobster coral.

He did the same for me.

'Some dinner,' I said.

It wasn't until we had eaten a second helping that she relaxed, leaning back in her chair and regarding me.

'Coffee,' she told the waiter as he cleared the dishes. 'A cigarette, please, Dirk.'

I gave her a cigarette from my pack, lit hers and mine.

'That's a lot better,' she said, and smiled at me. 'Now we can talk.'

The waiter returned with a pot of coffee, poured, then went away.

I waited, looking at her. She was too good to be true, I told myself. She had everything most women would envy and a saint would be unable to resist, but her glittering green eyes, as hard as emeralds, warned me this woman was very dangerous.

'So what do we talk about?' I asked, sipping my coffee.

'You are the first man I have met in this God-forsaken city who has guts. I need a man with guts.'

'What makes you think I have guts?'

'A man who can bomb a stinking hole like the Black Cassette and scare an ape like Smedley so he quits the city has guts.'

'How do you know he's quit the city?'

'Half an hour ago, he telephoned. He wanted to talk to J.W. I recognized his voice so I told him J.W. was tied up and what did he want? He said you had tortured him into telling you that Angela Thorsen had hired him to do the acid job, and he had to quit. Could J.W. give him money?' She paused, then went on, 'I told him to go to hell, and hung up. I got one of the boys to check. Smedley has gone, heading for Miami.'

I sat waiting, knowing there was a lot more to come.

'I haven't told J.W. what Smedley told me about Angela Thorsen,' she went on. 'She is valuable to him. If he knew she was behind the acid job, he would be sure you were going to fix her. You wouldn't last ten minutes.'

'All the same, I am fixing her,' I said.

'To understand this scene, Dirk,' she said, lowering her voice, 'I am going to wise you up.'

'Why?'

'I told you: I need a man of guts. Now I have found you, I don't want you blown away in your hunt for revenge. You can't buck the organization. Now, listen! J.W. is the top shot in Florida. His job is to collect money for the organization. Florida is a gold-mine. Anyone with money has a secret, and there are thousands of them who pay blackmail. The big stores, the casino, the top hotels pay protection money. J.W. lives at the Spanish Bay Hotel for nothing. The hotel doesn't want staff trouble. J.W. has only to raise a finger and the staff will walk out. The monthly take is big: around a million and a half. J.W. is responsible for keeping to this figure or increasing it. This makes him vulnerable. The organization would replace him if he began to slip. This is the reason why he is anxious to have no trouble in this city. He gets ten thousand from the Thorsen girl. If you start trouble for her, J.W. will be ten thousand short. I know the organization is getting dissatisfied with his work. They want a bigger increase. He is living on a tightrope. Let me tell you, Dirk, the only reason he hasn't had you blown away is that you are too well known here, and are friends with the cops. He doesn't want any publicty. You with me?'

'Why are you telling me all this, Sandra?' I asked. 'I understood you worked for J. W., and he seems to think a lot of you.'

Her smile was evil and bitter.

'I'll come to that. The only reason J.W. wanted to see you

117

was to con you into believing how sorry he was about the acid job. You accepted his story that Minsky was dead and buried. J.W. is a most convincing liar. Minsky is his right hand. It is Minsky, with his team of ferrets, who dig up the dirt for blackmail. Without Minsky, J.W. would be lost. He would no more think of getting rid of Minsky than you would cutting off one of your arms. Minsky is alive and working. Smedley is a bird-brain and useless to the organization. When he arrives in Miami, he will disappear. Minsky is an expert at making unwanted people disappear.'

I leaned forward.

'Are you telling me this sonofabitch who sprayed acid in my girl's face is alive?'

She nodded.

'That's what I am telling you.'

I drew in a deep breath, feeling cold rage run through me.

'Where do I find him?'

'You won't. You don't even know what he looks like.'

'He's short, broad-shouldered, wears a white coat and a broad-brimmed hat.'

'So what?' Her expression was cynical. 'He takes off his hat and white coat, puts on a grey coat and doesn't wear a hat. How many hundreds of short, broad-shouldered men walk about this city? You won't ever find him unless I help you.'

I stared at her.

'Why should you help me?'

Her face turned to stone and her green eyes narrowed.

'Because he murdered my father.' The words came in a hissing whisper.

'Why?'

'So J.W. could replace him. My father ran the Florida racket brilliantly. I was his secretary. We were very close.' She leaned back and motioned to me to give her another cigarette.

'You are a mafioso?'

'Of course, but, now, I am also a worm in the apple.

118

When my father died, I swore over his dead body to revenge him, and that's why I need a man of guts.' She leaned forward so I could light her cigarette. 'Two worms are better than one, Dirk.'

I was absorbing all this.

'You became J.W.'s secretary?'

'Yes. He had no idea that I knew he had ordered my father's murder. The killing was cleverly arranged: a hit-and-run driver in Miami. My father left me a letter. He knew J.W. was after his job, and he knew Minsky would kill him. I had been my father's secretary for more than three years, and I knew far more about the racket than J.W. did. He was only too happy when I offered to work for him.'

'Why did you do that? I would have thought you would have hated the sight of him.'

'The worm in his polished apple.' Sandra said with her evil smile. 'For more than a year, I have waited my chance. I knew I couldn't bring J.W. and Minsky down without help.' She stared fixedly at me. 'Now I have found a man of guts. With your know-how, I can revenge my father and you your girl. We have a common cause.'

'So what you are saying is that if Minsky is put out of action, J.W. will fall off his tightrope?'

'Yes. Of course, the racket won't stop. J.W. will be replaced. Someone like Minsky will continue to dig up dirt. No one can stop the organization, but we two could stop J.W. and Minsky. That would satisfy me.'

I thought about this. I didn't like the idea of working with a mafioso, but if it meant I could get at Minsky, I wasn't going to be fussy.

'Right,' I said. 'You can rely on me. What's the first move?'

She studied me with her hard, green eyes.

'You mean this, Dirk?'

'You can rely on me.'

She nodded.

'The first thing is to find Minsky. He reports to J.W. on

119

the phone. He's elusive. By now he'll have heard from Smedley, and he will know that Smedley has talked. But he won't know that you know he is alive. He could become careless. He won't return to his rented apartment. He rented it week by week. It was just a roof while he was in the city. The reason why Smedley lived there was a front. Someone had to pay the rent and live there. Minsky will have no trouble finding another roof. We'll have trouble finding him.'

'Do you think he could be holed up on the yacht *Hermes*?' She stiffened.

'Who told you about the *Hermes*?'

'I've been asking around, Sandra. Never mind who told me.'

'He won't be there. The yacht is only used as the pay-off station. J.W. only goes there on the first of the month. He collects the money, then sails for Miami. Yachts aren't Minsky's scene. He likes plenty of space.'

'How do you know?'

'My father told me. At one time Minsky worked for him.'

'You can give me a description of him, can't you?'

She shook her head.

'I've never seen him. I've only heard him on the telephone. He has a strong Italian accent.'

'He must have a girl-friend.'

She thought.

'Yes. Once when J.W. was talking to him on the phone, he asked how Dolly was. She could be Minsky's girl-friend.'

My mind switched to Dolly Gilbert, the whore, who lived at the Breakers condo. If she was Minsky's girl-friend, no wonder she was so frightened when I had mentioned Hank Smedley. Possibly, Smedley was cheating on Minsky and screwing Dolly. This was worth a long, careful look.

'Do you know where the new drop is going to be?' I asked, keeping my face dead-pan. 'Now the Black Cassette no longer exists, the blackmail victims will have to be told where to deliver their pay-offs.'

'I don't know, but I will find out.'

'Minsky is certain to show up on the first of the month to collect the blackmail money. We have eight days. Find out where the new drop is to be. I'll stake it out if I haven't found him first.'

'Yes.' She nodded. 'Leave that to me. I'll telephone you. Give me your number.'

'It's in the book. One more thing, Sandra, do you know why Angela Thorsen is being blackmailed?'

'No, I don't. Minsky keeps the records. All J.W. is interested in is getting the money.'

'You mean to tell me that J.W. has no idea of the names and the sins of the people from whom he gets a million and a half each month?'

'Why should he? He relies entirely on Minsky. He doesn't want to bother with details. He's running a big drug ring, and that keeps him busy. He leaves the blackmail racket to Minsky.' She looked at her watch. 'I must go. J.W. will be back soon.' She regarded me. 'I can rely on you, Dirk?'

'You can.'

'I have a charge account here. Give me five minutes,' and she started to move to the door, then paused. 'When you have found Minsky, don't kill him.' Her green eyes flashed, and again her face became as if carved out of stone. 'That is going to be my pleasure,' and with a wave of her hand, she left me.

When I left the Three Crab the time was pushing 01.00. There was nothing I could do until tomorrow morning. I drove home. Bill had already gone to bed, so I went to bed myself. I dozed fitfully, my mind busy with the facts Sandra had given me, but finally I slept.

Over a 10.00 brunch, I told Bill what I had learned.

Stirring his coffee, he looked questioningly at me.

'So what now?' he asked.

'I am going to fix Minsky,' I said. 'Then I'm going to fix

Angie. I want you to keep with Angie. I want to find out a lot more about her than I know now. Stick with her, Bill. Find out what she does. Where she goes. She just can't stay in the little cottage. I want to know who she meets, who she contacts. OK?'

'Sure, but what are you going to do?'

'I'm going to the Breakers condo to talk to the janitor. Maybe Minsky is holed up with Dolly. Whatever he's doing, wherever, I'm concentrating on Minsky.' I finished my coffee. 'OK, Bill, you stick with Angie. See you tonight,' and I left him to drive to the Breakers.

The time now was 11.00. I found the janitor in the basement, supporting himself on his broom handle and staring into space. His pig-like face brightened when he saw me.

'Ah, you again,' he said. 'Did you find Zeigler?'

'No. I'm looking for someone else. Have you see a short, thickset man who wears a white coat and a broad-brimmed hat?'

He leaned more heavily on his broom handle.

'I see a lot of people coming in and out of this dump.'

'I'm not interested in a lot of people: a short, thickset man who wears a white coat and a broad-brimmed hat.'

'Maybe,' he said and stared at me for a long moment. 'I could have seen him.'

I took out my wallet and produced a ten-dollar bill.

'This help your memory?'

He snapped the bill out of my fingers, kissed it and put it in his dirty sweat-shirt pocket.

'Yeah. He's Dolly's pimp. Comes here from time to time. I guess he collects money from her.' He moved the brush aimlessly in a sweeping movement. 'I ain't supposed to talk about people, living here, mister. They wouldn't like it.'

'They won't know about it if you don't tell them.'

He scratched his hairy arm.

'I guess you're right.'

'Give me a description of this man.'

122

'No, mister. He wouldn't like that. I wouldn't want to get in trouble with him.'

I produced another ten-dollar bill, folded it and raised my eyebrows.

He stared at the bill.

'That for me?'

'Could be. I want a description of this man.'

He thought, then nodded.

'Like you said. Short, tough-looking. I only saw him twice, and that was enough. His face looked as if someone had trodden on it when he was a kid: flat nose, sloping forehead: a face that would scare anyone.' Again he eyed the bill I was holding. 'That *is* for me?'

'His hair? Dark or blond?'

'I wouldn't know. He's one of these freaks who shaves his head. I guess that's why he wears a hat. He's as bald as an egg.' He continued to eye the bill I was holding. 'Shaved off his eyebrows too.'

At last! I thought, I now had something to work on. I gave him the bill.

'How often does he come here?'

The janitor shrugged.

'I wouldn't know. I don't often have the time to be in the lobby. He was here last night. I was putting the trash cans out when I saw him come in. For all I know he could be still with his whore.'

'OK,' I said. 'See you later,' and I left him. I climbed the stairs to Dolly Gilbert's apartment. I approached silently and cautiously.

Hanging on her door handle was a notice:

DON'T DISTURB.

I moved to the door, and with my ear pressed against the door panel, I listened. Faintly, I could hear voices: a man's voice, then a woman's voice. I guessed they were in the bedroom. I walked down the stairs, then out onto the street to where I had parked my car. I got in the car, lit a cigarette and prepared myself for a long wait. I had nothing else to do, and I was used to waiting.

I waited for two long boring hours, then as my watch showed 13.40, I saw Dolly come out with a short, thickset man following her. Dolly was wearing a paper-thin imitation leopard coat and a head scarf. I scarcely looked at her. My attention was riveted on the man.

Wearing a black sports cap with a long peak, a black windcheater and white slacks, I had no doubt that this was Hula Minsky. His hairless, brutal face was frightening. His broad shoulders, short thick legs, gave him the appearance of a savage gorilla.

Looking at him, knowing he was responsible for Suzy's death, I had to control myself not to pull out my gun and kill him.

He walked with Dolly a few yards, then stopped by a dark green Caddy, unlocked the driver's door and slid under the wheel. He let Dolly in on the off-side.

I started my car engine, waited until he had pulled out, then moved after him. He drove onto the lower end of Ocean Boulevard, then turned down a side-street and pulled up outside an Italian restaurant. The door man came fast across the sidewalk to open the car door. He saluted as Minsky got out. I drove slowly by. I watched in my driving mirror. Minsky and Dolly entered the restaurant.

I found parking at the end of the street and walked back on the other side of the street. I came on a sandwich bar and entered. I sat on a stool by the counter where I had a good view of the restaurant opposite. I ate two beef and pickle sandwiches and then ordered coffee. An hour later, and after I had had three more coffees, I saw Dolly come out and walk away, heading back to the Breakers. I paid my check, then wandered out onto the street. Passing the Caddy, I made a note of its number plate, then walked to where I had parked my car. I got in and waited, watching my driving mirror.

I had a half-hour wait before Minsky appeared. With him was a tall, thin man wearing dark glasses. He had on an open-neck shirt and jeans. His hair was long, reaching to his shoulders. He had on a black straw hat, pulled well down, screening his face.

The two men got in the Caddy. Minsky at the wheel, drove by me as I started my car engine. I waited until he reached the end of the street, then I drove after him.

At the end of the street, turning right, I came onto Seaview Avenue which was congested with traffic. No driver would give way to me, and after sitting, cursing, for over four minutes I realized I had lost Minsky. The lights changed and there was a break in the traffic. I drove onto Seaview Avenue, then cut to the Neptune Tavern. Spotting Al Barney, sitting on his bollard, nursing a can of beer, I parked right by him.

When he saw me, his fat face brightened. I slid out of my car.

'This is a quickie, Al,' I said, and stuffed a twenty-dollar bill into his dirty sweat-shirt pocket. 'A tall, thin man, long black hair, wears a black straw hat and sun-goggles. Who is he?'

Barney flinched.

'Poison. Keep clear of him, Mr Wallace. Sol Harmas. He handles Walinski's yacht.'

'Where do I find him?'

Barney looked furtively to right and left.

'You're going to be the death of me, Mr Wallace,' he muttered. 'He owns the last bungalow on Seaview Avenue. When he's not on the yacht, he's there.'

'Thanks, Al,' I said, got back into my car and drove towards Seaview Avenue. I had a long wait before I got onto the avenue. Cars were crawling towards the beach: girls in bikinis, boys in swim trunks, all car radios blasting pop. I finally drove slowly with them to the far end of the avenue which gave onto sand, palm trees and the sea.

As I crawled by, I took a long look at the last bungalow before the beach took over.

125

The bungalow was more like a ranch house. Maybe five bedrooms and a big living-room. It was protected by a high wire fence, and at the entrance gates two tough-looking men in white drill, guns on their hips, stood, chewing gum.

I pulled into a parking bay and waited until the boys and girls ran screaming and yelling towards the sea.

When there was a lull, I drove back slowly, again passing Sol Harmas's pad. This time, near the entrance to the place, I saw another man in white drill, leaning against a tree with a police dog at his feet.

I drove on, fairly certain that Hula Minsky was holed up in this heavily guarded place. To get at him, I thought, as I drove against the traffic, I would have to wait until he came out.

Finally, away from the traffic, I pulled up beside a call box and put a call through to the Spanish Bay Hotel. I asked to speak to Miss Sandra Willis.

'A moment, sir,' the girl said.

There was clicking, then Sandra came on the line.

'Who is this, please?'

'Can you talk?' I said.

'Quickly. He's on the terrace.'

'Can we meet?'

'Six o'clock. The Three Crab.' Then her voice hardened. 'I am sorry, you have a wrong number,' and she hung up.

I assumed Walinski had come into the room.

I returned to my car and did some thinking, then I drove to police headquarters.

I found Tom Lepski at his desk, scowling at a flimsy he was holding. Two other detectives were at their desks, hammering out reports.

'Hi, Tom!' I said and smiled at him. I pulled up a chair and sat, facing him. 'Busy?'

He gave me his hard, cop stare.

'Where were you last night around midnight?'

'If you must know I was stuffing my gut with a girl-friend.'

'Who? What's her name?'

'Come on, Tom,' I said. 'You know you can't ask a question like that. Why do you want to know where I was?'

He snorted.

'Just come in.' He shook the flimsy. 'Miami police report that they have fished the body of Hank Smedley out of the harbour. He's been shot through the back of his head.'

I felt a wave of satisfaction run through me: one down, now two to go: Angela and Minsky.

I put on my surprised expression.

'I wonder who did that?'

'Anyone but you, huh?'

'That's correct,' I said. 'Well, that ape is no loss. I looked in for information, Tom. First, have you found anything further about the acid job?'

He looked away from me.

'A dead-end. I'm sorry, Dirk. You know what we know, then nothing.'

'Know anything about Sol Harmas?'

'You mean who captains Joe Walinski's yacht?'

'That's him.'

'No record. What's he to you?'

'Tom, I'm not leaving this acid job alone. Suzy was my future wife. I'm collecting information, and when I have something concrete, I'll come to you.'

He nodded.

'Give us some evidence, and we'll go into action.'

'Harmas?'

'Lives in style. Has guards. We have nothing to pin on him.'

'Next question. What do you know about Hula Minsky?'

Lepski stiffened, staring at me.

'What's that bastard to do with you?'

'I am certain he was the one who used the acid spray. The description fits him, and he let Smedley run his apartment. The two of them fixed Suzy.'

'Proof?' Lepski demanded, leaning forward.

'Not yet, but I'll get it, then you'll get it.'

He shook his head.

'Look, Dirk, you don't know what you are walking into. Minsky is really dangerous. I know how you feel about Suzy. You're probably right that Minsky did the acid job. That's his style, but he's smart. You won't pin anything on him. Why not forget it? Smedley is dead. So, OK, you are more or less even. Keep out of this for crissake.'

'You do know that hundreds of citizens in this city are being blackmailed? Maybe you don't know the take is over a million and a half a month.'

He gaped at me.

'We know about the blackmail racket. As big as that? How do you know?'

'I have informers, Tom. They talk to me when they wouldn't talk to you. Now, listen. On the first of every month, the blackmail victims pay up. The big shots pay their money to Smedley. The small fry go to Walinski's yacht around three in the morning. Their money is collected there. At that hour, the waterfront is deserted except for the two waterfront cops who are in Mafia pay. Get rid of those two, and replace them with two sharp cops with the authority to question anyone wanting to go aboard Walinski's yacht. Could pay dividends, Tom.'

'Smedley's joint doesn't now exist. So what?'

'There'll be a new drop. I'll let you know where it is.'

Lepski took his hat off, ran his fingers through his hair, then replaced his hat.

'I'll have to talk to the chief.'

'That's what I want you to do. Let's have some action. The first of the month – another seven days.' I shoved back my chair and stood up.

Lepski stared at me.

'Leave Minsky alone,' he said. 'He's too big for you, and almost too big for us to handle.' Lowering his voice, he went on, 'There are many big shots in this city who would rather pay out than have their dirty lives exposed. Remember that!'

128

'As if I didn't know. Tell me, Tom, are your people doing anything to crack this blackmail racket?'

'A well-organized blackmail racket,' Lepski said quietly, 'is the hardest nut to crack. We do know Walinski handles it, but that doesn't mean a thing. We need three or four victims to complain to us, and then, and only then, can we start some action. Suppose we strike lucky? Suppose we get three or four men to admit they have done something bad, and are being blackmailed? They won't, of course, but if they did, they would be fished out of the harbour like Smedley before we could get them to court.'

'So you're doing nothing?'

'That's about it, Dirk. We're doing nothing.'

'Change those waterfront guards. You could upset this blackmail thing.'

'I'll talk to the chief.'

'See you, Tom,' I said, and left him.

I had time to return home. Bill wasn't there. I guessed he was watching Angela Thorsen, which might be boring but shouldn't be too strenuous, so I didn't feel too conscience-stricken in doing something I hadn't done in years, it seemed – put my feet up, shut my eyes, and thought of nothing, except maybe a lot of black sheep jumping over a very high fence. Much refreshed, I took a quick shower, changed, and then drove to the Three Crab Restaurant. I arrived three minutes to 18.00.

I was welcomed by Wally, the *maître d'*, who flashed his teeth at me.

'Miss Willis is waiting for you, Mr Wallace,' he said. 'You know your way up?'

At this hour the restaurant was alive with waiters, laying tables and generally preparing for the dinner-time rush.

I nodded, climbed the stairs, knocked on the door and found Sandra sitting at the table, cigarette between her slim fingers.

129

'Hi, Dirk!' she exclaimed. 'This has to be a quickie. He's only out until seven.'

I sat down opposite her.

Again I was more aware of her sexual vibes. She looked stunning in a sky-blue dress, and her green eyes were hard and calculating.

'I've seen Minsky, and I think I know where he holes up,' I told her.

This produced a big reaction from her. She leaned forward, her green eyes flashing.

'You've *seen* him? How?'

Briefly, I told her what the janitor had told me, how I had seen Dolly leave with a short, broad-shouldered man, wearing a sporting cap, how I had followed them to an Italian restaurant, and then when Dolly had left, the man I was sure was Minsky had come out with another man.

I told her this man was Sol Harmas. The two had driven along to Seaview Avenue where I had lost them.

'Yes!' She exclaimed. 'That's where he is! The ranch house! J.W. had the place built at my father's suggestion. It's security proof. There's no way of getting at Minsky so long as he's there – not a chance!'

'So, OK. We wait. He'll come out, then we go into action.'

'He's certain to come out on the last day of the month, then we go into action. Yes, that's when we get at him.' Her smile was the most evil thing I ever hope to see on a woman's face.

'You haven't seen him. I have. When he shows, what do you suggest?'

'We grab him. I want him alive. I want him to suffer.' Her face was again like a stone mask.

'I've seen him. Grabbing Minsky would be like trying to catch a tiger with a butterfly net.'

She got to her feet.

'There are always means. I'll think of something. J.W. is going to New York for three days. We meet here on Thursday.'

Thursday would be the day before the first of the month.

I nodded.

'OK – here.'

She nodded, then, patting my shoulder and giving me a small, hard smile, she left.

I sat for some moments thinking, then I went down to where I had parked my car and drove home.

8

It was well after 22.00 when I heard Bill unlocking the front door. I had spent time, a glass of Scotch in my hand, doing some heavy thinking.

The rain had set in, and I could hear it beating against the windows. I got to my feet as he came rushing in, ready to make a stiff drink for him, but one look at his face, as he stood in the doorway, his mac shining with rain, made me pause.

'Don't say a word!' he exclaimed. 'I want to eat! I want a steak as big as your desk! Come on. Let's go!'

'Calm down, Bill. We have things to talk about.'

'That's what you think. I'm starving. For eight hours, I've been sitting in the rain with only a hot dog to eat. I've had it up to here! We don't talk: we goddamn eat!'

Knowing Bill, I put on my mac, locked up, then went with him to his hired car.

It wasn't until forty minutes later, in which time Bill had demolished a king-sized steak smothered with fried onions and a stack of french fries, that he began to look human again instead of a starving refugee.

I had been nibbling at a crab salad, watching him. When I saw he was beginning to relax, I said, 'So it's been rough, Bill. Anything to report?'

'Not yet,' he said, and ordered a double portion of apple pie.

So I waited with growing impatience.

Finally, finished, he sat back and grinned at me.

'Man! I certainly wanted that!'

'I asked you if you had anything to report,' I said, at the end of my patience.

'Sorry, Dirk, but I was starving,' he said. 'Yes, plenty to

report. I've been watching Angie's cottage since eleven o'clock this morning. I didn't see a sign of her. Around midday, Mrs Smedley came out with a shopping basket and took off in the Beetle. Then ten minutes later Angie appeared. It was raining quite hard. She was wearing the jeans and sweat-shirt and the big sun-goggles. She began to walk around the garden, getting soaked. From where I was sitting in the car, a good hiding-place, I could look down on her. She paced around the garden like a caged wild cat. I could faintly hear that she was talking to herself. Every so often, she would stop and bang her head with her clenched fists. It was an unpleasant sight. Two or three times, she would shake her clenched fists in the air, then go on walking and talking to herself. She behaved as if she was out of her mind. Then she returned to the cottage, slamming the door.

'I sat there. Then Mrs Smedley returned, carrying a heavy shopping basket. Nothing happened for the next two hours, then action really started. I heard hysterical screams coming from the cottage. The screams really got to me. They were eerie and blood-chilling. I rushed down to the cottage and looked through the living-room window. Man! What a scene! Mrs Smedley was in a corner and Angie was creeping up on her. She had a big carving knife in her hand. Mrs Smedley looked calm. She was talking. Then Angie screamed, "I want you out, black bitch! I want Terry!"' He paused, then went on, 'This set-up looked straight out of a horror movie. There was this crazy-looking girl with the knife, edging towards Mrs Smedley who was pressed against the wall. I ran to the front door and leaned against the bell. Angie who was still screaming she wanted Terry, stopped screaming. I kept leaning on the bell. After some minutes, the door opened and Mrs Smedley, her face running with sweat, glared at me.

'"Excuse me," I said. "I'm from the *Reader's Digest*. I was wondering . . ." I got no further. She slammed the door in my face. I waited a minute or so, then peered through the living-room window. Angie was sitting in a chair, hammering her head with her clenched fists. The knife was lying on the floor. Mrs Smedley picked it up and took it into the kitchen. Then she came back and caught hold of Angie. She gave her slap across her face that seemed to knock Angie unconscious, then she carried her out of sight. So I returned to my car and sat and waited, but there was no further action. Well, that's it, Dirk. Angie is a real nut-case and should be put away.'

'She kept screaming for her brother?'

'That's it.'

'Josh told me the sun went out of her life when her brother left. What's happened to her brother? Where is he? I've felt all along Terry is the key to unlock the puzzle.'

'So, OK. What's the next move?'

'I'm going to talk to Mrs Thorsen. She's the only one able to certify Angie. The two people who could give real information are Josh and Hanna Smedley. Sorry, Bill, but you get back to watching the cottage. I'm going to Thorsen's place. With luck I'll be able to talk to Mrs Thorsen.'

Bill groaned.

'If you say so. OK. Then let's go.' As we were leaving the restaurant, he asked, 'How long do you want me to watch the cottage – all night?'

'You nose around, Bill. See what's going on. I'll join you after I've seen Mrs Thorsen. Stay right there until I arrive.'

We got into our respective cars and headed for the Thorsen residence. I parked some yards from the gates while Bill drove up the narrow lane to the cottage.

As I walked up the drive in a fine drizzle of rain, I saw the big house was in darkness except for a light in Josh Smedley's room.

Mrs Thorsen was obviously out. I hesitated for a long moment, then decided I would again talk to Josh. The time was 21.30. Maybe she would be returning soon, I thought, as I pulled the bell chain. I had to do this four times before the door opened.

134

Josh stared at me.

'The detective gentleman?' I said. 'Mrs Thorsen is out.'

'I want another talk with you, Josh,' I said, and shouldered my way into the lobby.

Passing me, he plodded unsteadily down the corridor to his room. I could see he had been hitting the bottle hard. He entered his room and sat down. There was a bottle of Scotch and a half-full glass on the table beside him. He folded his black hands in his lap and regarded me with glazed eyes.

'You heard about Hank?'

'Yes, Mr Wallace. Well, I warned and warned him, but he only laughed at me. He thought he would be looked after. I pray he is now at peace.'

'You have told me that Terry and Angie were very close,' I said. 'Tell me just how close.'

'I don't understand, Mr Wallace.'

'Think about it, Josh. How close?'

'She worshipped him. When he went to the music room to play, she would sit on the stairs outside the door and listen. That's how close.' He shook his head sadly, then took a gulp at his drink. 'When Mr Terry left home, she changed. She became difficult. My wife was the only one who could handle her.'

'I am working on the theory that because her father made life impossible for Terry and drove him away, Angie, in her mental state, decided that if her father was dead, Terry would come back home. Do you agree with this thinking?'

He moved uneasily in his chair.

'I don't know what went on in Miss Angie's mind.'

'I think Angie deliberately stirred up a quarrel with her father, a violent quarrel, bad enough to bring on a heart attack, and then pushed him so that he fell, striking his head.'

He sat motionless, staring into space.

'You heard what I said, Josh. I think Angie killed her

135

father so her brother could return home. I think someone saw it happen and that is why she has been paying blackmail, Josh, through Hank Smedley, your son.'

He heaved a heavy sigh, looking up at me from under heavy brows.

'You are wrong, Mr Wallace. I have to tell you, you are wrong. There was a quarrel, a violent one, but Miss Angie went away before her father collapsed. Only I saw that happen. I heard their angry voices but when I went in he was alone and struggling to get his tablets from his desk, the tablets he had to take in a bad attack. I saw him and he saw me. I found the tablets.'

'Yes?'

'I found them and took them away. He collapsed, and his head hit the desk. I didn't touch him. I went out. When I came in again I found him like I told them. Dead, and that is how I killed him.'

I stared at him for a long moment.

'Do you know what you are saying, Josh? *You* killed Mr Thorsen?'

He nodded.

'Yes, sir, I say I killed him, because I let him die.'

'But why?'

He sat still, staring into space, then he said, 'It goes back a long time, Mr Wallace. I have served Mr and Mrs Thorsen for some thirty years. When she married, I came with her. I was a good butler. Mr Thorsen was pleased with me. It wasn't until my son was born that my troubles began. Hank was always in and out of real trouble. I asked Mr Thorsen if he would let Hank take care of the garden. He agreed, and gave him a small salary. For a time, Hank liked doing the garden, and he did it well. He seemed to be settling down. Then Miss Angie began to fool around with him. She was about 13 years of age. Hank was 26. It got serious, Mr Wallace, and Mrs Thorsen found out. Hank was sacked. From then on Hank was in constant trouble with the police. He had six months in jail.'

Josh paused to sip his drink. 'Then my wife and I began to quarrel: always about Hank. This so upset me, I began to drink. I guess I got hooked. Then, one day, Mr Thorsen sent for me. He told me I had been so long in their service, he was leaving me five thousand dollars in his will. That may not seem to you a big sum, but to me it was a fortune. Time passed with Hank always in trouble and I drank more and more. Then Mr Thorsen found me drunk. He gave me notice to quit and at the end of the month, and he told me he was cutting me out of his will. This was a terrible blow to me. As I've told you, Mr Thorsen was a hard man. To leave this lovely house . . .' He lifted his shoulders in a despairing shrug. 'Then Hank came to see me. He told me if he could get five thousand, he would be able to open this club. He asked me if I could give him the money. I told him I had no money like that. He said not to worry, he would rob a bank. I was sure if he did that he would be caught and spend years in jail. I told him to wait a few days. I guess I hit the bottle hard. If Mr Thorsen died, I would continue with my job as butler and I would be able to give Hank the money he wanted. Mrs Thorsen would never give me notice to quit. So when Mr Thorsen died as I have told you, with Miss Angie coming in like the hand of providence, I kept my job and got the money. It was a bad thing to do. Hank's now dead.' He regarded me with glazed eyes. 'My only wish now is also to be dead.'

I got to my feet. I didn't want to hear any more. Looking at this wreck of a man, I felt sorry for him.

'The coroner's verdict was "natural causes",' I said. 'I've already forgotten what you have told me. So long, Josh. I won't be seeing you again.'

He sat there, staring at the Scotch in his glass. I didn't know if what I had said had sunk into his drink-sodden brain. I had the feeling his wish would soon be granted.

I left him like that and walked down the long drive in the drizzling rain to where I had parked my car.

* * *

The lights of Paradise City made a rainbow of colour against the sullen, rain-swollen clouds. I wasn't impressed. I had seen it all before. I stood by my car, listening to the distant roar of the traffic, watching the headlights as cars moved along the boulevards.

I unlocked the car door and dropped into the driving seat, out of the drizzle. I sat there thinking of Josh Smedley. What a loving father would do for a worthless son! I shrugged. I now wanted to see Bill and to hear if anything was happening at the cottage. As I was about to start the car engine, I heard a sound that made me pause. The sound was an ambulance siren that grew louder, and a moment later an ambulance followed by a car swept by me and turned into the narrow lane leading to the cottage. I caught a glimpse of two men in the car. Knowing Bill was up there, I decided to stay put and not confuse the situation. I lit a cigarette and waited. It was a long wait. Some forty minutes later, I began to lose patience, then a chauffeur-driven Rolls swept by me. I saw Mrs Thorsen sitting at the back. The Rolls turned into the narrow lane. I decided to keep out of it. I lit yet another cigarette and waited. Another dreary half hour crawled by, then I heard the ambulance siren start up. Moments later, the ambulance appeared and went racing off towards the city, followed by the car with the two men. I guessed they were doctors.

I still waited, then after twenty minutes the Rolls appeared and drove towards the Thorsen's residence.

I started my car engine and drove up the narrow lane. From time to time, I flashed my headlights to alert Bill I was on my way.

As I approached the gate to the cottage, I saw Bill who waved to me. I pulled onto the grass verge as he ran to my car. He slid into the passenger's seat and slammed the car door.

'Go ahead, Bill,' I said. 'Tell me.'

'I saw the action through the living-room window,' Bill said. 'Man! Plenty of action! I guess I arrived at the right

138

time. Mrs Smedley was sitting. I felt sorry for her. I guess she was trying to decide what she would do. After a time, I saw the living-room door slowly open and Angie appeared. She had got hold of the kitchen knife again. She began to creep towards Mrs Smedley. She looked out of her mind and vicious. I never want again to see anyone looking like that. She gave me the horrors. I was about to break the window and yell to Mrs Smedley when she must have sensed her danger. For a woman built like a Jap wrestler her reaction was impressive. As Angie was coming at her, Mrs Smedley was on her feet, had the knife away and gave Angie a clout that knocked her across the room. She then pounced on her and carried her into the bedroom, out of my sight.

'She was out of sight for a good ten minutes, then she returned to the living-room, picked up the telephone receiver and dialled. I guess she was calling for help, and believe me, she certainly needed help. Then Angie began screaming again, but I guess Mrs Smedley had tied her up. She kept screaming she wanted Terry. Mrs Smedley's phone call got a lot of action. In twenty minutes, an ambulance . . .'

'I know,' I said. 'I saw them arrive. What happened?'

'They brought Angie out on a stretcher and away they went. Then Mrs Thorsen arrived. She talked to the two doctors, then they left. While this was going on, Mrs Smedley stood, leaning against the wall, listening. Mrs Thorsen started talking to her. I couldn't hear what she was saying, but from the expression on her face what she was saying wasn't pleasant. Then she opened her handbag, took out two 500-dollar bills and threw them on the table. That's it, Dirk. It's my guess Mrs Thorsen told Mrs Smedley to pack up and go.'

'OK, Bill. Stick around. I think this could be the right moment to talk to Mrs Smedley.'

I left the car. It had stopped raining, so I took off my mac and threw it on the back seat of the car, then I walked to the front door of the cottage. I pressed the doorbell, then, finding the door unlocked, I entered the small lobby, then walked into the living-room.

Mrs Smedley was sitting in a heap in an armchair. She looked up, stared at me, then nodded.

'You! What do you want?'

She didn't look or sound hostile so I sat down in a chair near hers.

'You have been told by Mrs Thorsen to pack up and leave. Is that right?'

She nodded.

'That's right, and I'll be glad to go. I have had enough of the Thorsens. I'm going back to my people. For the first time in twenty years, I feel free to do what I like.'

'I am glad for you,' I said in my most soothing voice. 'Before you go, Mrs Smedley, will you tell me about the Thorsens? I want to know why Angie was being black-mailed. Do you know?'

She stared at me for a long time while she was thinking; then she shrugged her massive shoulders.

'Yes,' she finally said. 'I guess I need to talk to someone before I leave. I want all this off my mind before I return to my people. I have four brothers and three sisters. They'll all welcome me. I come from a big family. If it wasn't for Miss Angie, I would have gone to them years ago. I nursed Miss Angie from the moment she was born. I knew she was a little crazy. I helped her a lot. I did everything for her, and she loved me for it. Her mother never did a thing for her. Miss Angie worshipped her brother. They got along fine together until he began to grow up, then I saw he was getting tired of her. She wouldn't leave him alone. I warned her, but she wouldn't listen. Then he started this piano playing. He would lock himself in the music room and she would sit outside, listening. She was mad about his playing. Then he and his father had a quarrel. Mr Terry left home. He didn't even say goodbye to Miss Angie. It was a terrible shock to her, and from then on, she became more and more crazy in the head. I had a bad time with her, but I did manage to control her. Then Mr Thorsen died suddenly and left her all this money and this cottage. She moved into it at once. She hated her mother. She did nothing. She would sit in a chair all day, staring and muttering to herself. I guess I made a mistake. I should have told Mrs Thorsen to get a doctor, but I disliked Mrs Thorsen, and I hoped to pull Miss Angie out of this mood, so I kept trying to get her interested in the garden, to do something around the home, but she took no notice. This went on for a week and I was making up my mind to get help when a man arrived.'

Mrs Smedley paused to wipe away the sweat that was running down her face. 'He didn't ring the bell. He just walked in. I was in the kitchen, preparing dinner. He sat where you are sitting and took off his hat. He was completely hairless and had the face of a devil. I was just coming out, when I heard him say he knew where Terry was, so I waited and listened. Miss Angie completely changed. She became alive. "Where is he?" she demanded. This man told her her brother didn't want anyone to know where he was. He was being a success with his piano playing. He told Miss Angie her brother sent her his love. Then the business. This devil of a man told her her brother was under his protection. "I don't protect people for nothing," he said. "I want you to go to the Black Cassette club on the first of every month with ten thousand dollars. As long as you continue to do that, your brother will be protected by me. If you don't, someone will break your brother's hands with a hammer, and he will never play again. You have the money. I have the protection".'

Mrs Smedley paused again to wipe the sweat off her face. 'This was ten months ago. Miss Angie said she would pay. This devil of a man told her where to find the Black Cassette. He said all she had to do was to walk in with the money on the first of every month. She would find an old friend, waiting. The old friend was my no-good son. May he never have been born!' She thumped her knees with her clenched fists. 'I tried to talk to Miss Angie. She wouldn't listen. I tried to warn her this man was a bluffer. I said it wasn't likely he did know where Mr Terry was. She wouldn't listen. She kept screaming, "To break those wonderful hands with a hammer." So every month, she went to the bank, got the money and gave it to my no-good son. Doing that seemed to give her more peace of mind. She wasn't so difficult. There was nothing I could do about this, so I just looked after her.

'Then, soon after, this hairless man came again. I listened from the kitchen. He said if Miss Angie gave him a hundred thousand dollars, he could fix it for her to meet her brother. Then you came, telling her you were looking for her brother because he had inherited a hundred thousand. You told her all he had to do was to go to the bank and they would pay him. Miss Angie wanted this money so she could see Mr Terry again. Into her crazy mind came the idea of finding someone to impersonate Mr Terry, get the money, and she would give it to this hairless man and finally see her brother. She went to Hank who found someone. You know what happened. She came back here in a terrible state. She behaved like vicious, wild animal. She scared me. I shut myself in the kitchen. She kept screaming, "I'll fix that sonafabitch. He must have a girl-friend. I'll talk to Hank. I'll fix him good." Then she left in her car. I didn't see her for three or four hours. When she returned, she was much calmer. "I've fixed him," she told me. I had no idea what she was talking about until I read in the paper about the acid attack.' She shuddered. 'I'm sorry, but she's not in her right mind.'

I thought of Suzy: the acid, the pain, the truck smashing into her.

'And Angie?' I asked. 'What's going to happen to her?'

Mrs Smedley lifted her vast shoulders in a gesture of despair.

'She's being put away in a nut-house – they call it a mental clinic. I listened while the two doctors talked to Mrs Thorsen. They said Miss Angie was beyond recovery.

There was no hope for her. The only thing to do was to keep her under drugs and locked up. Mrs Thorsen told them to go ahead. Miss Angie now might as well be dead.'

There was nothing more I wanted to hear: nothing more I wanted to know. I got to my feet.

'If there is anything I can do to help you, Mrs Smedley, just tell me. I have a car outside. Can I drive you down to the city?'

She stared at me, then shook her head.

'I don't need anyone's help. Go away! I'm going back to my people.'

I left the cottage, and stood for some minutes in the garden, feeling the humid heat and hearing the distant sound of the traffic.

Hank was dead. Angie was locked away for life. Two down: one to go.

Hula Minsky!

I knew I would never rest until I had fixed that hairless ape. When that happened, this cold fury inside me for revenge might die. Suzy might become a wonderful memory. Stupid hopes? Could any revenge blot out Suzy's last moments of life?

I walked to where Bill was waiting.

'We'll go home and talk,' I said.

I got in my car. He got in his and we drove to my apartment.

Bill made coffee while I gave him the complete picture about Angie and Terry and Minsky, but about Josh I had given my word, so I kept my mind and my mouth shut.

'Well, there it is, Bill,' I said. 'Tomorrow I see Sandra. All I'm interested in is to fix Minsky. I'm going to bed.'

I stunned myself to sleep with three sleeping-pills.

It was while I was finishing a solid brunch breakfast that Bill had prepared that the telephone bell rang.

The time was 11.15. Both of us had slept heavily. The sound of the bell made me wince.

I picked up the receiver.

'Dirk Wallace,' I said.

'This is Sam, Mr Wallace, the Neptune Tavern. Mr Barney wants to see you. He says it's important.'

'Where is he, Sam?'

'He's here, having his breakfast. He says he'll wait.'

'I'll be along in twenty minutes. Thanks for calling, Sam,' and I hung up.

I told Bill.

'You stick around,' I said. 'I'm off.'

'Hold it,' Bill said, a snap in his voice. 'I'm sick of sticking around. I'm coming with you. I'll stick around in the car if I'm going to stick around anywhere.'

So, leaving the breakfast debris on the table, we went down to the garage and I drove to the Neptune Tavern.

Leaving Bill in the car, I crossed the waterfront and entered the tavern. I found Al Barney seated at his special corner table, wiping his plate clean with a piece of bread.

I sat in a chair opposite him. He regarded me, then nodded.

'You want breakfast, Mr Wallace?' he asked.

I said I'd already had breakfast and did he want a beer?

'I never say no to a beer, Mr Wallace.' He signalled to Sam who came racing over with a beer and a plateful of the lethal sausages.

After he had swallowed half the beer, he set down the mug, wiped his mouth with the back of his hand, threw into his shark-like mouth three of the sausages, then relaxed back in his chair.

'Mr Wallace, I am a man with his ear to the ground. I don't ask questions. I listen. So OK. You told me you were interested in Terry Zeigler. So I listen. You still interested?'

'Yes, Al,' I said.

He threw three more sausages into his mouth, chewed, grunted, then leaned forward, his peppery breath fanning my face.

'The man you want to talk to is Chuck Solski. He was a

144

drug pusher before the Mafia took over. From what I hear Zeigler was a close pal of his. Solski needs money. If you spread some dollars in front of him, he'll tell you what happened to Zeigler. You'll find Solski at No. 10 Clam Alley, top floor. That's the best I can do. OK?'

'Thank, Al.' I took out my wallet, but he waved it away.

'We're friends, Mr Wallace. I don't take money from friends.'

I shook his clammy hand.

'Thanks again, Al.'

I returned to my car where Bill was waiting. I told him what Al Barney had said.

'I'll see if this guy is home.'

'Clam Alley? That's at the far end of the waterfront. It's a condemned slum. I'll be surprised if anyone is living there. The few apartment blocks are going to be torn down.'

'How do you know?'

Bill gave a sly smile.

'Barney isn't the only one who keeps his ear to the ground. No point in walking. We'll drive.'

With Bill at the wheel, we drove slowly along the waterfront, now packed with tourists. Finally, he pulled into a parking slot.

'Clam Alley is just ahead.'

'You certainly know this district,' I said as I got out of the car.

He walked with me.

'I'll stick around, Dirk,' he said. 'That's No. 10 facing us.'

Clam Alley was the worst slum I have ever seen. There were four five-storey blocks. Every window in these blocks was smashed.

The door to No. 10 hung drunkenly open on one hinge. I edged into the filthy, stinking lobby, littered with rubbish. Bill followed me.

'For God's sake!' I exclaimed. 'Surely no ones lives in this cesspit.'

145

Facing me were stairs.

'Al told me he's on the top floor,' I went on.

'Watch it, Dirk,' Bill said. 'Those stairs look rotten. You could break a leg.'

I started up the stairs that creaked as I climbed. The door to the first apartment hung open. It was empty and filthy. I climbed to the second floor. The same empty apartment. The third floor was the same. Whoever had lived in these hovels had gone. Finally, with Bill behind me, I reached the top floor. The stink of the place was stomach-turning. Facing me was a door that was closed: the only door in this ghastly building that was closed.

I rapped on the door and was greeted with silence. I rapped again, still silence. I tried the door handle and the door creaked open. I moved cautiously into a small attic room. Bill remained outside, looking through the open doorway.

I've seen slums in the Negro quarters in West Miami, but nothing like this dreadful little room. It contained a packing-case to serve for a table, two stools and a bed. The litter of past meals, newspapers, and other muck covered the floor. The room was a hell-hole of squalor.

Lying on the bed was a man. He lay on sheets that hadn't been washed in years. The man and the bedding matched the awful squalor of this room.

I moved towards him, paused by his side and stared down at him. He was wearing a pair of filthy, tattered jeans. He was as thin as a skeleton. His matted black hair fell to his shoulders. His beard hid most of his face. At a guess, I thought he was around 35 years of age. He gave off the body stink of a man who hasn't washed in months.

He seemed to be sleeping.

I hated to touch him, but I took hold of his arm and gave him a violent shake.

'Hey! Chuck!' I bawled in my cop voice. 'Wake up!'

His eyes snapped open and he stared at me, then he swung his spindly legs off the bed onto the floor.

'Who the hell are you?' he demanded, his voice husky. He was now sitting upright.

'I'm a guy with money to spend,' I said, stepping away from him. 'I want information from you.' I took out my wallet and produced two one-hundred-dollar bills. 'These interest you?'

He stared at the bills as if I was showing him all the gold in Fort Knox.

He ran his fingers through his matted hair. I kept well away. I didn't want to collect any of his lice.

'Jesus! I want money!' he muttered. 'I need money!'

'I need information, Chuck. We can do a deal.'

'What information?'

'Are you OK? You don't look it. Can you think straight?'

He sat there for several minutes, staring down at the filthy floor. I could see he was pulling himself together. Then, finally, he looked up and nodded.

'I sleep a lot,' he said. 'There's nothing for me to do but sleep. When I sleep, I hope I won't wake up, but I still do. I always wake up and find myself in this goddamn hole. I haven't the guts to jump into the harbour. At the end of the week, they are coming to knock this rat-hole down. I don't know where I am going. I've come to the end of my line, but the goddamn line won't finish.'

'Chuck, I want information from you, and I'll pay two hundred dollars for it.'

'What do you want to know?' He regarded me. 'You ain't a cop, are you?'

'No. I want to find Terry Zeigler.'

He sat there, scratching his awful mop of hair while he continued to stare at me.

'Why?' he finally asked.

'That's not your business, Chuck. I'm offering you two hundred dollars to tell me all you know about Zeigler and where I can find him.'

He grimaced.

'Is that right? Suppose when I tell you, you spit in my face and walk out with the money?'

I tossed a hundred-dollar bill into his lap.

'You'll get it, Chuck, so start talking.'

He fondled the bill.

'Jesus! I need this,' he muttered. 'Know something? I haven't eaten for three days.'

'Start talking about Zeigler,' I barked. 'Come on, Chuck. The stink in this room is killing me.'

So he started to talk.

I sat on the packing-case that served as a table and listened.

He told me he had met Terry at the Dead End Club. They became friends. As he was on the needle himself, he realized that Terry was also hooked. This made a bond between them. Chuck was trying to promote a money-making drug business. He could get the stuff, but he failed in pushing it. He talked to Terry about this who said he was willing to try. During the afternoons, Terry would go out and sell the stuff. He was a big success. He had many contacts with the kids. They all loved his piano playing. Between them, Chuck and Terry, they worked up a flour-ishing business. Chuck got his supplies from an old Chinese, Terry sold the stuff.

'It looked super good,' Chuck said, vigorously scratching his head. 'We were both making money. I had a nice pad and lived on my own. Women have never interested me. Terry had a good pad and he had Liza, his girl-friend, to live with. Then, just when we thought we were set, we ran into a real problem. As usual, on a Monday, I went to my supplier to get more of the stuff. I walked into his office and found Hula Minsky at the desk.' He paused, then went on, 'Do you know Minsky?'

'I know,' I said. 'Skip him. So . . ?'

'The sight of that ape scared the shit out of me,' Chuck said, and shivered. 'OK. I'm on the needle and I have no guts. He told me my drug racket was finished. He said to tell my pal to lay off pushing – that was Terry. I was so scared of him, I would have kissed his feet if he had told me to do it.' Chuck ran his filthy hand through his filthy beard. 'I knew Terry was with Liza. I telephoned him and told him what Minsky had said. Terry said not to panic, but we would get together. He said he was coming to my pad. He moved in with a couple of suitcases. We talked it out. The supply had dried up. I couldn't afford to pay for my pad. We both had blown our money away. I told him I would have to move out. He said we must look for another supplier. He didn't give a shit about Minsky. I told him I was through. You don't buck an ape like Minsky.

'Terry said he would find another supplier. I didn't want anything to do with it. Terry was stubborn. He kept saying the hell with Minsky. I warned him, but he wouldn't listen. I remember him staring at me. He said he had more than fifty kids waiting for their fix. He wasn't going to let them down. I told him the hell with the kids, but he wouldn't listen. He said he had got these kids on the needle and he was going to feed their habit. He said he couldn't do anything else. I gave up. He took off, and he found another Chinese who could supply him. He got the stuff and sold it to the kids. I knew something would happen. I wouldn't have anything to do with it. I wouldn't take any of the money he made. I am so gutless, I just sat in my pad, shivering with fright. This went on for a week, then it happened. I knew it would. I kept warning Terry. He was telling me how much money he had made, and the new supply would be at the end of the week, when the door was kicked open and there was Minsky with two thugs. It happened so fast, I don't remember what did happen. I was lying on the floor, covering my head with my arms. There were awful noises: bones breaking: horrible noises. That was the end of Terry. I had warned him. Then Minsky kicked me. He said as I had done what he had told me to do, I could forget it. He said I was lucky to be alive. Then the door slammed. I got up and looked around. Terry was gone.

I had warned him. You don't fool around with an ape like Minsky. You want to know where Terry is? My guess is his smashed-up body is in a cement overcoat and at the bottom of the sea. They smashed him to bits and took what was left of him away. There was nothing I could do. I hadn't any money. I moved into this God-awful room. It was for free. I'm waiting to die. That's what I want – to die.'

I had no compassion for this derelict creature as I had for Josh Smedley. A mindless jerk who could make a profit selling heroin to kids deserved everything that came to him.

I stood up, dropped the other one-hundred-dollar bill on the bed beside him and joined Bill, waiting in the corridor. We made our way cautiously down the rotting staircase and into the fresh, humid air.

As we walked to our car, Bill said, 'I heard all that. I guess that takes care of Terry. The Thorsens certainly produced a couple of beautiful children.'

I paused to unlock the car door.

'It happens. The Thorsens weren't exactly beautiful parents either.'

We got in the car and sat for a long moment in silence, then Bill said, 'OK. Hank is dead. Angie is locked away. Terry is dead. That leaves Minsky – right?'

'That's it,' I said. 'Up to now we have had it easy, but Minsky won't be easy. In a couple of hours, I'll be seeing Sandra. I want to hear what she has got lined up. Tonight is the night for action.' I started the car engine. 'Let's go home.'

Wally, the *maître d'* of the Three Crab Restaurant welcomed me with his flashing smile.

'Miss Willis is expecting you, Mr Wallace. You know your way.'

I nodded, climbed the stairs, knocked on the door and entered.

Sandra was sitting at the table. Before her was a large cocktail shaker and a spare glass.

'Hi, Dirk!' she exclaimed. 'Help yourself,' and she waved to the cocktail shaker.

I sat down, facing her.

'Not right now,' I said, regarding her.

She was in white and her thick black hair fell to her suntanned shoulders. Her green eyes sparkled as she stared back at me. I decided she was the most sexy, evil-looking woman I hope never to meet again.

'And – so?' She poured herself another Martini from the shaker. 'What have you to tell me?'

'J.W. will be short ten thousand dollars on the pick-up,' I said.

She stiffened.

'How and why?'

Briefly I told her about Angie Thorsen.

'No more money,' I concluded. 'Your people can't threaten a woman in a mental clinic.'

She leaned back in her chair and released a hard, metallic laugh.

'This will topple J.W. The organization will fold him up and replace him.'

'I don't give a goddamn about J.W.,' I said. 'I'm only interested in Minsky.'

'Yes.' she grimaced. 'I've been checking. He's a rat who knows how to take care of himself. I wanted to get him to myself and kill him by inches to repay the death of my father, but this now is not possible. When he moves, he has bodyguards. There is only one way to fix Minsky. I have an automatic gun. I'm going to rip his filthy guts out with bullets. It's the best I can do.'

I shook my head.

'No. I don't like it. It is suicidal. You don't imagine his bodyguards will let you get away with this. You kill him. OK, I can see you can take him by surprise, but the bodyguards are certain to kill you.'

She gave me her evil-looking smile.

'No, Dirk. They won't dare touch me. Every member of

151

the organization knows me or knows of me. They know I am J.W.'s right hand. J.W. is in New York. He will be returning tomorrow night. When he hears I have killed Minsky he will turn his thumb down, but by then I will be a long way out of his reach. I've already packed. As soon as I have fixed Minsky, I take off. I'll get lost, and the organization won't find me. You don't have to worry about me. If there is one thing I can do well, it is to look after myself.'

Looking at her stone-hard face and those green ruthless eyes, I nodded agreement. If anyone could look after herself, it was Sandra Willis.

'Dirk,' she went on, 'you said you too wanted to get even with Minsky. I want you to finger him for me. You've seen him. I haven't. I don't want to shoot the wrong man. All you have to do is point him out to me – that's all.'

I hesitated for a long moment. If I did this, it would make me an accessory to murder. Then I thought of Suzy. This brutal sonofabitch who had sprayed acid in her face had to be fixed.

'No problem, Sandar,' I said.

'The new drop is now Fu Chang's restaurant,' Sandra said. 'Minsky will be arriving to collect the loot around three in the morning. We'll make sure of it. I'll be in my car. I want you to be there. We'll be there at two. So, OK, we will have a wait, but he just might be early. You finger him for me, and that's all I want. I'll handle the rest of it. OK?'

I got to my feet.

'I'll be there,' I said. 'I only hope your thinking is right.'

She picked up the cocktail shaker and poured herself another Martini.

'My thinking is always right, Dirk,' she said. 'See you at two tonight. I'll be in a Mercedes. I'll be parked by the restaurant. All you have to do is to tell me which is Minsky. OK?'

'I read you,' I said, and left her.

I joined Bill in the car.

'Fu Chang's restaurant?' I asked as I slid into the passenger's seat.

Bill snorted.

'On its way out and fast. It's a corner building on the east side of the waterfront. It started well, then Fu Chang, who must be shoving 90, lost his grip. Why the question?'

'That's the new drop.' I then went on to tell him of my talk with Sandra. 'That's the set-up, Bill,' I concluded. 'At two o'clock this morning, we park as close as we can to Fu Chang's joint. Sandra will be there in a Mercedes. I'll join her. When Minsky arrives, I'll finger him for her, then she blows him away. You stay put. If this works, she will take off, and we'll go home, but if it doesn't work, we give her covering fire.'

'If she kills Minsky and gets away, do you think we can go see the colonel and get our jobs back?' Bill asked. 'I mean, will you feel you have settled accounts for Suzy?'

I thought for a long moment, then nodded.

'I guess so. Once I'm sure Minsky is dead, then you and I will go back to work.'

'Fine. Now, let's go eat.' He started the car engine and drove me to Lucino's special lobster and steak dinner. We ate in silence. Both of us were absorbed in our thoughts. As we ordered coffee, Bill said, 'Do you think this is going to work?'

I lit a cigarette and pushed my pack to him.

'This woman is very special. I think it will work, but if it doesn't, and she gets shot, then I am finishing the job. She says the bodyguards won't dare to touch her. We'll see. It depends on her. There's still time for you to duck out, Bill. This isn't your private war.'

He looked at me, then finished his coffee.

'Don't talk crap, Dirk. Let's go home. We have three hours before action stations. I could do with nap.'

As we drove along the waterfront, I spotted two young, tough-looking cops, patrolling. Lepski had got some action. These two could make a dent in Walinski's pay-off.

When we got home, Bill went at once to his bed. I spent the next hour cleaning and loading our revolvers, then I too, dozed in an armchair.

At 01.45 I woke Bill, gave him his gun, and we drove back to the waterfront. Bill directed me.

'That's the dump,' he said. 'To your right.'

Fu Chang's restaurant had certainly seen better days. Now it looked almost derelict. A few dim lights showed through the dirty windows. There seemed no activity. Above the door to the entrance there was a bright light, shining on the road as if in hope someone would be tempted to have a meal in there.

At this hour parking was easy. I pulled into a slot some thirty yards from the restaurant.

'We could be in for a long wait, Bill,' I said as I cut the engine.

'That's what we are good at, isn't it?' he returned and settled himself in the car's seat.

As we watched, shadowy figures began to appear out of the darkness and then entered the restaurant: all kinds of people, mostly Cubans, some Chinese and a number of whites. They were in and out in seconds, and disappeared into the darkness. They were victims of the blackmail racket, paying their dues. There seemed a continuous stream of them.

A few minutes after 02.00, a small Mercedes arrived.

'Here she is,' I said. 'OK, Bill, we'll give her covering fire if there's trouble. You stay here. I'll go to her.'

'If there is trouble, Dirk,' Bill said as I slid out of the car. 'Do we shoot to kill?'

'If we don't, we'll get killed. This sonofabitch just has to be fixed.'

I walked the few yards to where the Mercedes had parked. She was sitting at the wheel. In the darkness I could just make out her silhouette. I opened the car door and got in beside her.

'Hi, Dirk!' she said. 'The big deal! I see the suckers are already arriving.'

154

'Is this going to work, Sandra?' I asked.

'It will work.' There was a note of finality in her voice. 'Just relax, and we'll wait.'

So I sat by her side, inhaling her exotic perfume while we watched people going and coming out of the restaurant.

We sat in silence for the next half hour. To me, she was a stone woman. I felt she didn't want to talk. From time to time I fingered the butt of my gun. I had never killed anyone, but tonight I was ready to kill.

I thought of Suzy. I thought of her last moments of life. Those terrible moments, blinded by acid and being crushed by that truck. If Sandra couldn't finish the job, then I would!

'Here they come,' Sandra whispered.

A big Cadillac came out of the darkness with only parking lights. It stopped outside the restaurant.

Four men spilled out: big, tall, each with a gun in his hand. It was like watching Cagney's old gangster movies. The men spread out, looking to right and left. I already had my gun in my hand. Then Minsky appeared. He looked almost a dwarf against his bodyguards.

'That's him,' I said. 'The little punk.'

'Thanks, Dirk.' She got out of the car, slamming the door.

The sound made the four bodyguards look in her direction. Without hesitation, she walked to where Minsky and his guards stood, staring towards her.

'Minsky?' Her voice was clear and sharp. 'I am Sandra. I have a special message for you from J.W.'

Then she appeared in the hard, overhead light.

What a performance! No hesitation and her looks! I've never seen a woman look so glamorous. She was wearing a scarlet and beige dress that clung to her. Her glossy black hair lay on her naked shoulders. She looked as if she had walked out of a *Vogue* photograph.

The four bodyguards lowered their guns and gaped at her.

I slid out of her car, keeping in the darkness. I looked across to my right and saw Bill was also out of my car.

The bodyguards moved back and Minsky stood there under the hard overhead light. He was staring at Sandra, then his ape-like face lit up.

'You Sandra?' he said. 'What's biting J.W.?'

'He has a special message for you,' she said.

In the stillness of the humid night, I could hear her hard, metallic voice.

'So, OK, babe. What's the message?'

She was carrying a big evening handbag. She was now within six feet of him.

'I have it here.'

The bodyguards had moved further back as Sandra zipped open the handbag. Her movements were so professional and fast, Minsky didn't stand a chance.

While Minsky was leering at her the gun was in her hand and she was shooting. At that range, Minsky got four bullets in his guts blowing him apart.

The four bodyguards just stood motionless. I lifted my gun, ready to give her covering fire, but she continued to handle the situation.

'OK, boys,' she said. 'J.W. wanted him off the scene. Get rid of him before the cops arrive.'

One of them, less thick in the head, said, 'If you say so, Miss Sandra.'

She paused for a few seconds to look down at Minsky as he lay, bleeding and dead. Then turning, and without hurrying, she walked back to her car.

It was a cold-blooded, beautifully staged performance.

I opened the door of her Mercedes and she got into the driving seat.

'You see, Dirk? My thinking is always right. You get the hell out of this before the cops come.' She looked searchingly at me through the open car window. 'This evens the score, doesn't it?'

'Yes,' I said.

She started the car engine.

'You've seen the last of me.'

'Watch out, Sandra. The Mafia has a long arm.'

She gave me her evil little grin.

'And I have long legs.'Bye.' She shot the car away and went fast from the waterfront.

In the distance, I could hear police sirens. I paused long enough to see the four bodyguards snatch up Minsky's body and throw it into the trunk of the Cadillac, then I ran to my car where Bill was sitting at the wheel. As I scrambled in, he took off, cut down a dark alley that brought us to the highway. He reduced speed and drove towards my home.

He said nothing.

Angie, Hank and now Minsky had been taken care of, I thought. There was nothing more I could do to level the score, but I knew for years I would think of Suzy, once so full of life and zest and fun, now so terribly dead. Nothing I had done would bring her back. Nobody would ever take her place.

It wasn't until we had walked into my living-room and shut and locked the front door that Bill said, 'Quite a woman! That scene was highly professional. Let's go to bed.'

'Yes,' I said. 'The job's finished. Thanks, Bill.'

He looked at his watch.

'It's after five,' he said. 'Let's have a damn good sleep, and a damn good brunch, then we'll see the colonel and get our jobs back.'

'OK,' I said.

He regarded me for a long moment, then he said, 'Dirk, you have to forget it. No one should live in the past. It's the future that matters. Tomorrow is a new day. Come on, let's go to bed.'

In the big double bed, with the dawn light coming through the curtains, I thought back.

Revenge?

Hank gone, Angie locked away, Minsky gone.

I put out my hand and caressed the pillow by my side where so often Suzy's lovely head had rested.

I didn't sleep. I lay there watching the sun slowly rise, flooding the room with golden light.

Bill was right. I could not live in the past. I thought of what he had said, 'Tomorrow is a new day'.

With that thought in my mind, with my hand still on the empty pillow by my side, I did eventually fall asleep.